LAST SUMMER
A SUMMER BOYS NOVEL

LAST SUMMER

A SUMMER BOYS NOVEL

HAILEY ABBOTT

SCHOLASTIC INC.

New York Toronto London Auckland Sydney
Mexico City New Delhi Hong Kong Buenos Aires

ISBN 13: 978-0-439-86725-2
ISBN 10: 0-439-86725-8

ALLOYENTERTAINMENT

Produced by Alloy Entertainment
151 West 26th Street
New York, NY 10001

SCHOLASTIC and associated logos are trademarks and/or registered trademarks of Scholastic Inc.

Text design by Steve Scott
The text type was set in Bulmer.

12 11 10 9 8 7 6 5 4 3 2 1   7 8 9 10 11 12/ 0

Printed in the U.S.A.
First printing, May 2007

"Congratulations, graduates!" cried the principal of Martin High, directly into the microphone. The sound reverberated out from the small stage and echoed across the June morning, over the heads of the seniors sitting in rows across the football field, and back up over the stands where the parents sat, applauding wildly.

On cue, the entire graduating class let out a long cheer. They weren't allowed to toss their caps in the air, or they'd have to pay a penalty fee, but one brave — or crazy? — soul did just that.

Beth Tuttle knew it had to be her ex-boyfriend, George.

But, whatever. Beth tilted back her head and let loose a banshee howl of her own. Then she reached over and hugged the kid nearest her: Michael Tutweiler, to whom she had previously spoken exactly once in their entire twelve years of Martin, Massachusetts, public schooling. It had been at graduation rehearsal one week ago, and had consisted of exactly four words: *Is this my seat?*

But Beth didn't care. And neither did Michael. The moment was bigger than either of them. She and Michael cheered wildly and pounded each other on the back.

"We did it!" Beth cried.

"We rock!" Michael replied at the same volume.

Then they let go of each other, and Beth grinned as Michael was swallowed up in the black-gowned crowd of seniors all around them.

Never to be seen again, she thought, *except maybe ten years down the road at a class reunion*. Somehow, though, she was okay with that. Michael Tutweiler would be her private graduation-day memory.

Beth pulled the black mortarboard hat from her head, shook her shoulder-length blonde hair free, and sighed.

High school was over.

After a moment, she turned to follow the chaotic surge of her classmates back across the football field and toward the brick school building, where their families waited on the wide school lawn.

"Tuttle!" One of Beth's younger swimming teammates

launched herself at Beth. "What are we going to *do* without you next year?"

"Kick some ass," Beth replied with a smile. "Life'll go on, I guess."

The other girl looked like she couldn't imagine that, but Beth was already moving on, picking her way through the crowd of celebrating new graduates, looking for her parents.

Life *would* go on, Beth mused. She would meet new people; maybe become a new person herself — as if the eighteen years that had created the person she was right now were just a *base* for everything that would come after.

Beth was leaving for college in August. She knew that going to college meant changing her whole world. She'd watched her cousin Kelsi change in a major way this past year at Smith College. Beth watched the CW Network. She knew that high school was where people dreamed about things, and college was where people actually *did* them.

She almost wished she could go straight to college, without having the summer to wait and wonder about it. She wanted her future to begin *now*.

"Bethy!" cried her mother, and then Beth was swept up into her arms. Her mother couldn't stop hugging and congratulating her. Her father stood to the side and snapped picture after picture: Beth with her mother, Beth with her diploma, Beth grinning and holding on to her braided gold tassel. Beth knew it was only a matter of time before these pictures were in frames all over their house.

"Okay," Beth said when her eyes were dizzy from the flash, and her jaw was beginning to ache. "I have to return my cap and gown or they'll charge me."

"We're so proud of you, sweetheart," her mother said with a big smile, and then kissed Beth on the cheek. Beth hugged her mom back, hard.

"Take as much time as you need," her father told her in a gruff voice.

Beth felt a surge of emotion as she looked at her parents, and tried to imagine *not* living with them anymore. She was an only child, and she had a relationship with her parents that was kind of different from the ones she knew her friends had with theirs. She knew it was dorky, but she *liked* hanging out with them sometimes. So thinking about going off to college and leaving them felt a little bittersweet.

"I'll see you guys in a bit," Beth murmured, feeling like she should say more, but not knowing how. The way her parents smiled at her, she thought maybe they understood.

She turned then, and headed away from them.

The past several months had been like this, Beth thought, making her way through the crowd once more. Different. Strange. Surreal. If she thought back to this time last year, it was like thinking about an alternate reality. She'd been Beth Tuttle, but a completely different version of herself.

A year ago, she'd still been with George. He'd been more than a typical boyfriend — he'd been Beth's best friend. They'd inhabited a little world that was all about the two of them. Their own games, secret nicknames, a whole private language of jokes, dreams, and silliness. As Beth walked down the hallway of her school, she shook her head. She'd had no idea that last summer would tear them apart — that Beth would do the tearing herself — or that they'd break up for good at Thanksgiving.

Beth would have assumed, a year ago, that losing George would kill her. It nearly had, last summer. Then the autumn had arrived and they'd grown so far apart, and she felt like she needed to lose George completely in order to really live.

It still hadn't been easy. It was like she had transferred to a new school these last few months — that's how different things felt without George. But she'd concentrated on her college applications. She'd spent Christmas visiting her cousins, Ella, Kelsi, and Jamie, who were like sisters to Beth. Instead of treating the prom like a big romantic thing, Beth had gone with a big bunch of single girls — and they'd had a blast. She'd kept on swimming. She'd run track. She'd gotten into college.

"I did it," Beth said out loud then, attracting the notice of one of the parents near her. She smiled when the man looked at her, mostly because she saw that he was the father of Steve Wilson, captain of the soccer team, and one of Beth's old friends.

"Congratulations," Steve's father said to her politely, which made Beth want to giggle.

"Thank you," Beth said very formally. She had to bite back a laugh at the look on Steve's face, as his mother took what had to be the zillionth photo of him in his cap and gown.

"*Mom*," Steve complained, "I have to find my friends."

When she heard that, Beth admitted to herself that it felt the tiniest bit weird to finally be at graduation day without George. Well, not *without* him. She'd heard his name called during the ceremony, and it had surprised her how much she wanted to cheer and scream for him. Since she hadn't really wanted to *see* him in the past six months, it was a change.

Beth shrugged it off, then ran down the flight of stairs that led to the auditorium. Inside, the chaos was extreme. Kids were lining up to return their graduation outfits, but were using their last moments as classmates to branch off into groups, sign yearbooks, and make promises about staying close.

"Beth Tuttle! Come over here and sign my yearbook!" called a guy who Beth knew from track. His name was Paul, and he had the distinction of being both the tallest and fastest kid in their class.

"I have to return these," Beth called back, indicating her cap and gown with one hand.

"Don't think you can get out of it," Paul warned,

pretending to brandish his yearbook at her. "Remember, I *will* catch you!"

Beth was laughing as she turned back toward the line, and she definitely wasn't paying attention.

So that was how she bumped into George.

Literally bumped into him. Like, with her entire upper body.

They both shot their hands out to steady themselves, and then dropped their hands abruptly when they saw who they'd collided with. It looked practically choreographed.

"Hi," Beth said, diving right into the awkwardness. "Sorry. And, uh, congratulations."

"You, too," George said immediately, and more politely than she remembered him ever being. He ran a hand through his wild dark curls.

"Guess you made it after all," Beth said, trying to smile, though it felt a little forced. Because they'd joked a long time ago that the numerous Enemies of George might bar him from participating in the graduation ceremony, simply out of spite.

Beth had a weird thought. Maybe *she* was one of the Enemies of George now. How depressing was that? She felt anxiety pool in her stomach. This was *exactly* why she'd been avoiding him for months.

George gave her a half smile. "Yeah. What a relief."

"Uh-huh. So, what are your plans?" Beth asked quickly,

aware that her face felt a little heated. She was embarrassed to be asking *George* such stiff questions, like they were strangers.

But maybe that's what they were now. Strangers. It occurred to Beth that George probably didn't know what her actual life plans were either. Because why should he?

"Oh, you know," George said airily. "World domination, battling evil, an occasional dragon slaying, the usual. You?"

"Nothing quite as exciting as your Xbox," Beth said, feeling a spark of her old wit as she raised her brows at him. "I'm going to Georgetown in the fall."

George looked at her for a moment, and then his eyes warmed with that wicked humor she hadn't seen in a long, long time.

"That just proves my theory, you know," he told her.

"I'm afraid to ask what you mean by that," Beth said, rolling her eyes in the way that only George could make her roll them.

"You shouldn't be afraid, Beth. After all, you can't help it. It's only natural."

"Help *what*?" she demanded.

"Once you go George, you never go back," George said happily. "I'm going to enjoy thinking of you wearing Me Town sweatshirts for the rest of your life."

Beth shook her head at him, but she couldn't contain her grin. "How about you?" she asked. The *George*town irony had nagged at her ever since she'd gotten her acceptance letter.

"After much consideration," he replied solemnly, "I decided that Pittsburgh, Pennsylvania, will be the lucky recipient of all that is George come fall. I'm going to Pitt."

"Cool." Beth nodded. She'd guessed that George might go there, since his older brother had as well. "What are you doing this summer?" she asked then, pleased that their conversation felt more normal now.

"It's funny you should ask." George pulled his graduation gown off, and folded it messily in his arms. Beth did the same, and they stepped into the returns line together. "My friend Dean —" He paused. "You don't know him — we painted houses together last summer. He invited me up to his grandparents' place, for a summer of total relaxation. It's a cool little town in Maine. You might have heard of it. Pebble Beach?"

Is this really my life?

"It sounds familiar, yes," Beth said drily.

George looked at her, then away. When he spoke again, his voice was lower.

"I didn't want to just, like, appear in Maine. That's your place. I wanted to respect that." He shrugged. "I kept wanting to talk to you about it, but it never seemed like the right time."

"Things have been weird," Beth acknowledged.

"This is pretty much the first conversation we've had

since . . ." George shrugged again. It was like he didn't want to admit that it had been cold outside with snow on the ground the last time they'd spoken. Neither did Beth. "In a long time."

"Things have been *really* weird," Beth clarified.

"Yeah, they have."

They stood next to each other in the slow-moving line, quiet for a moment.

Beth thought about how tense and strange it had all been — the months of not talking to him, not sharing everything with him. Not sharing *anything*. She'd pretended not to see him in the halls. Ignored him in their classes. Acted as if they'd never had a history.

Which seemed kind of silly, now that it was all over. Now that high school was over, and everyone had to move on to something new, what did the past matter?

"I think you should go," Beth said, tossing her hair back. "Pebble Beach wouldn't be Pebble Beach without you."

She almost said, *Look what happened last summer*, but thought better of it just in time. Why would she want to remind George that she'd fooled around with that lifeguard?

"Are you serious?" George asked, his dark eyes searching her face.

"Of course I'm serious," Beth said, not sure if she meant it entirely, but wanting to come off as the bigger person. "I don't think you should avoid the nicest place on the Maine coast just because I'll be there. Pebble Beach isn't *that* small. We might not even see each other."

"Like you could stay away from Ahoy Bar and Grill," George said, shaking his head at her. "I was having this recurring dream where you stumbled over me sitting at one of the booths." He shuddered. "Not pretty."

"Ahoy by definition is not pretty," Beth replied. "Try crowded and crazy."

"You love it there," George teased her.

"Can't deny it," Beth agreed.

They got to the head of the line, and had to split to their separate ends of the alphabet to return their armloads of graduation attire.

"Guess I'll see you in Maine," George called out, lifting a hand.

"See you," Beth called back, still dazed by the direction her summer had taken.

So much for normal.

Kelsi peeked out the window for the eighty-seventh time in three minutes, but the driveway in front of her mother's Colonial-style house remained empty. The suburban Connecticut street at dusk looked exactly the same as it had always looked throughout the entire course of her childhood: the lawns well-manicured, the houses serene, the yards festooned with oak and linden trees.

And no sight of her boyfriend's car.

She propped herself up on her knees and turned around so she could see herself in the mirror across the room. She assured herself that she still looked as cute as she had when she'd gotten ready, hours ago. Her short hair was glossy and nut-brown, and she'd outdone herself with lip gloss, thanks to a panic attack and a trip to Sephora earlier in the day.

Kelsi was not normally the lip gloss type, but she thought a reunion with her boyfriend deserved something a little more special than her usual Burt's Bees lip balm. Paired with her new favorite flowy halter top from Anthropologie and the Chip & Pepper jeans her fashionista sister, Ella, had given her for her birthday, Kelsi thought she looked exactly like the Bohemian princess she aspired to be.

If only Bennett would hurry up and arrive, so he could fully appreciate it.

Kelsi flopped back against the cushions on the couch and let out a rueful sigh. She was *almost* embarrassed for herself. She was glad her mother was away for the weekend, and that her sister had gone to her boyfriend's place in Philadelphia, so there was absolutely no one around to watch Kelsi run to the window over and over again. She'd completely lost her cool — and all because of a boy.

Nothing about Bennett had been what she'd expected. That was one of the reasons Kelsi had fallen in love with him in the first place. She certainly hadn't expected it to be so hard, not being with him for the eternity between the end of finals and the middle of June, when the Tuttles headed up to Maine and summer officially began.

But now the wait was over.

Kelsi took a few deep, calming breaths, and thought back to where everything with her and Bennett had started.

She'd had the most amazing first year at Smith College.

A year ago, she'd felt so lost and worried about her future. Now that she knew how it all turned out, she couldn't believe she'd been so stressed out. Hindsight was definitely 20/20.

For example, Kelsi couldn't have known that instead of finding herself awash in homesickness and fear like many of her classmates at Smith, she would, by pure coincidence or the grace of the housing gods, find herself living with Taryn Gilmour.

The thought of her irrepressible, pixie-like, irreverent best friend made Kelsi smile as she shifted into a more comfortable position against the soft cushions.

Taryn and Kelsi had fallen into a friendship quickly, but unlike many other friendships they'd watched crash and burn throughout the year, they had only gotten tighter. So tight that Taryn had been thrilled when Kelsi started dating her brother, Bennett, who went to school at nearby Amherst College.

Though not as thrilled as Kelsi had been, of course.

Kelsi couldn't have predicted that what had seemed like such a great relationship with hot, snarky Tim from Pebble Beach would turn out to be just a summer thing. Back in Maine, Tim had seemed to transcend his frat-boy roots. At school, though, it turned out that Tim really *did* enjoy all those keg stands and drunken toga parties. It wasn't that he had turned into a different person, necessarily. It just seemed that he and Kelsi had both emphasized other parts of their personalities when they'd met each other. Maybe Maine had brought out the best in them, Kelsi thought charitably. But dating while Kelsi was at Smith and Tim was at UMass had made their essential differences entirely too clear.

Kelsi had broken up with Tim just before Thanksgiving, in the middle of midterms. When she'd returned to school, it seemed like Taryn was on a mission to help Kelsi discover what she'd been missing while she'd been occupied with Tim.

"There's a whole world of men out there," she'd told Kelsi in her knowing drawl. "Not all of them think the pinnacle of life is a packed keg party with half-naked girls. Some of them like art. Books. Music, even."

Taryn felt that her artistic brother was the perfect person to usher Kelsi through this new, collegiate world of Men Who Liked Other Things. The three of them went to a Pedro the Lion show over at Amherst one weekend. Then the next weekend, they road-tripped around the area to check out local galleries for a paper that Bennett was writing in his art history class. One afternoon, just Kelsi and Bennett had driven into Boston to watch the entire Krzysztof Kiesowski's *Three Colors* trilogy. As they headed back home, Kelsi's head was filled with French cinema and Bennett's delightful raspy voice, as they talked about films and ideas the whole way.

It was probably right then that she'd fallen in love with him, with winter racing by outside the windows and all that warmth and sexy intellect inside the car.

But it wasn't until a few weeks later that things really happened between them. Kelsi had found out that the Smith Studio Art department was having a Make Your Own Art night. She'd invited both Taryn and Bennett, but only Bennett was free. They'd laughed and laughed as they'd collaborated on their first sculpture: a metal and wood rendition of Taryn — all edges and motion. Later, they'd walked across the Smith campus in the dark, crunching their way over the frozen ground with their breath coming out in puffs. Kelsi couldn't remember what they'd talked about that night. She just remembered the big moon overhead, and how soft and perfect Bennett's lips were when he finally leaned close and kissed her.

Taryn had loved the fact they'd gotten together only slightly more than she'd loved the sculpture, which she'd placed in the center of Kelsi's and her room for the remainder of the school year. The three of them were like their own little family unit these days.

The best part was that Taryn had agreed to spend the summer in Pebble Beach with Kelsi and the assorted Tuttles. It would be like having another cousin to hang around in Maine with, and Kelsi couldn't wait. She imagined the two of them sprawled out on the beach, gleaming in the Maine sunshine, and she just knew that the rest of her family would love Taryn the way that she did.

Kelsi thought that Ella, particularly, would adore Taryn. Especially since Kelsi's sister would get to spend the summer on the old sunporch that doubled as a guest room. Whenever the sisters shared the bedroom — which was every past summer — they spent half their time fighting. Thanks to Taryn, Ella would finally get what she wanted: her own space. The thought of the inevitable Taryn-Ella bond, and the havoc they would wreak, should have scared Kelsi, but instead it made her laugh.

"Anybody home?"

At the sound of that familiar, beloved voice, Kelsi jack-knifed into a sitting position and let the rush of joy sweep through her body. It was always this way. Every time she opened her eyes and saw Bennett, she felt like she glowed.

"Did I leave the front door unlocked?" she asked, drinking in the sight of him from her spot on the sofa.

"You did," he said, "and I walked right in. This is not the safety-conscious girlfriend I thought I knew, Kelsi. I'm disappointed."

He was nothing of the kind, as the mischievous glint in his eyes attested.

"You took a very long time to get here," she chastised him, still not moving, still wanting to soak in the anticipation of his nearness. She wanted to prolong the separation, so it would be that much sweeter when she reached out and touched him.

Kelsi studied Bennett as he stood there in the entryway to the family room, looking slightly disheveled from the road. She hadn't known it was possible to love every single cell of someone else's body. She loved Bennett's slightly messy, slightly longish coppery-red hair, and the emo-kid cut he wore it in. She could sink into his warm, intelligent dark eyes behind those adorable Buddy Holly glasses. She loved the stretch of his arms and the way his butt looked in his hipster jeans. She loved the way his smile seemed to light up his whole body, and the way he cocked his head slightly to the left when he aimed that smile at her.

"I had to make a few stops," Bennett said, and then Kelsi couldn't take it any longer.

She bounded to her feet and threw herself across the room, connecting with his body in a big bear hug that swept him back a few feet and brought her up on her toes. Finally close to him, Kelsi could smell the warm scent of his skin. She closed her eyes and just inhaled him. He smelled like sun and heat and Bennett. Like love.

"I missed you," she murmured, her eyes still closed.

"These were some tough weeks," Bennett agreed. Kelsi opened her eyes as he pulled back slightly and grinned down at her. Then he lowered his head and kissed her, his lips hot and soft and familiar. The kiss grew in intensity, and they were both a little breathless and giddy when Bennett pulled away again. "But I have a surprise for you."

"Who needs a surprise?" Kelsi protested when he pulled even farther away, breaking all contact except for his warm hand around hers. "You're here!"

"You'll love it," he assured her, and tugged her along behind him into the hall, where Kelsi saw he'd stashed a picnic basket. "Everyone's away this weekend, right?" he asked in a low voice. Kelsi nodded. "Excellent," he said.

Bennett led Kelsi down the hallway, out the back door, and into the warm Connecticut night. In the center of the backyard, he let go of her hand, and set about creating a ridiculously romantic nighttime picnic right there in the grass near her mother's rhododendrons.

Kelsi could only stare and then laugh in amazement as he shook out a blanket, and set out tea candles in adorable little lanterns all around it, bathing the blanket in a soft, romantic light. When he was finished, Bennett held his hands out to Kelsi, and pulled her inside the ring of light he'd created.

"First, dinner," he said as they sat down together on the soft blanket. "Then I want to talk to you about something."

The picnic hamper was filled with all of Kelsi's favorites — roasted eggplant sandwiches and vegan potato salad, olives and cherry tomatoes, with brownies for dessert. Kelsi was sure it was the best meal she'd ever eaten. As they ate, Bennett told her stories about his recent art projects and his father's well-meaning, if bumbling, attempts to understand things, such as finding his only son half naked in the basement at two A.M., covered in purple paint.

"I think he'd have been a lot happier if I'd been covered in beer," Bennett told her, laughing. "You know, *beer* he could comprehend. He was the president of his fraternity back in the day. Me — all wild-eyed and clutching my paintbrush? Not so much."

"What did he do?" Kelsi asked. She put the remains of her brownie aside (dairy- and gluten-free, because Bennett was good at details, she thought happily), and stretched out on her back, her feet across Bennett's lap so she could see the stars. It was only the stars above and this little ring of light, with the two of them in the center. And Bennett's sweet, deep voice, which she felt she could listen to forever.

"He hemmed and hawed and left me to it," Bennett said. "Which is the most you could ask for, I think. Right?"

"Definitely," Kelsi agreed. She'd met Bennett and Taryn's parents several times, and was always struck by how normal they seemed in comparison to their madcap children. How the four of them handled one another so well was one of life's great mysteries.

"So that's kind of what I wanted to talk to you about,"

Bennett said gently, moving her feet aside and stretching out next to her.

"Purple paint at two A.M.?" Kelsi laughed at him. "I don't think I need any further details to enjoy *that* visual!"

"Very funny." Bennett propped his head up with one hand, and Kelsi stopped laughing as his gaze went serious behind his glasses. "Do you remember me talking about Carlos Delgado?"

"Carlos Delgado," Kelsi echoed, as if she had to think about it. She wrinkled her nose. "I think I might have heard you mention him five or six thousand times. Since he's only your favorite contemporary artist in the entire world . . ."

"So, you remember," Bennett said drily.

"I'm still not sure," Kelsi teased him. "I remember going to Manhattan for the weekend and visiting his gallery show no less than seven times. But besides that, I don't think I remember."

"So there was this internship," Bennett said quickly. Kelsi got the sense that his excitement was too unwieldy for him to even respond to her teasing. "And one of the seven times we went to the gallery, I picked up the application, and don't be mad, Kels, but I decided to apply." He let out a breath.

"Why would I be mad?" she asked, shaking her head at him.

"Because I hid it from you." Bennett reached over and traced a pattern slowly along her arm, up her neck and to her cheek, as if she were his canvas and his finger were a paintbrush. "I thought that if I pretended it wasn't real, it would hurt less when I got rejected. Is that crazy?"

"It makes perfect sense," Kelsi told him, turning her head to kiss his palm.

"But the most amazing thing happened," he whispered. "And now I'm afraid that it isn't real, but I'm going to tell you, anyway."

"You got it." She knew from the sparkling wonder in his dark eyes, and the joy in his voice.

"I got it." Bennett stared at her, shaking his head. "I'm going to be Carlos Delgado's personal assistant for the whole summer."

Kelsi let out a little whoop of joy, and grabbed him into a hug.

"This is terrific!" she cried. "I'm so proud of you!"

"I'll visit you every weekend, or maybe you'll come down," Bennett added hurriedly, hugging her back. "I don't want you to feel like I'm blowing off our summer together —"

"We'll work it out," Kelsi assured him, cutting him off with kisses. "This is going to be the best summer ever. You're going to learn so much!"

"I can't believe it," Bennett confessed. "I mean, that's

actually true, I'm not just saying that. I'm *incapable of comprehending* that I'm going to be spending day after day with my idol. I can't get my head around it!"

"You're an amazing artist yourself," Kelsi said staunchly. Not only because she loved Bennett, but also because it was true. "Someday someone's going to say the same thing about you."

"I think maybe you're biased," Bennett said with a laugh, and they kissed out there under a canopy of summer stars.

They kissed and kissed, rolling back and forth on the soft blanket, and once again Kelsi thought about how special and safe Bennett always made her feel. She knew that she wanted to stay with him forever. She knew it deep down in the pit of her stomach. She knew it in her fingers and her toes. She knew it with every breath she took and every blink of her eyes.

Which was why she decided, as she felt love course through her in waves, that she wanted to *really* be with him. The way they never had been, in all the time they'd been together.

"Hey," she whispered, smiling up at him in between kisses. "I want it to be tonight."

"You want what to be tonight?" he asked, gazing down at Kelsi with tenderness.

That was just one more reason to love him, Kelsi thought, her smile widening.

Unlike every other guy she'd ever dated, sex wasn't the first, last, and only thing on Bennett's mind.

"If you want to," she went on, feeling suddenly a little bit shy, "I'd really like to . . ." It was ridiculous that she was going to be a sophomore in college and didn't know what to call it. "Sex" seemed so scientific. "Making love" was just a weird thing to say and she couldn't speak it without cracking up. In her head it was just . . . *It*.

The *It* that she hadn't done, despite being pressured by every guy before this one.

The *It* that she'd thought about so much and worried about so much, and now it just seemed like the obvious thing to do. The right thing, even.

"Oh," Bennett said in a hushed voice, getting what she meant. They looked at each other.

"What do you think?" she asked. Because it wasn't just her choice. It would be the first time for both of them, if it happened.

Kelsi suddenly wanted it to happen, so much so that she thought she might be shaking.

"I think," Bennett said slowly, carefully, "that it would be perfect."

They both laughed again — nervous and excited and hopeful laughter. Kelsi helped him blow out all the candles and then they climbed to their feet and she led him inside, up the stairs to her old bedroom. Once inside, they kissed again, long and sweet. Again and again, as if they were relearning how to kiss each other. Their bodies pressed together tight. As they kissed, they pulled off each other's clothes and then they were naked, and then they were in the shelter of Kelsi's bed.

"Do you want to change your mind?" Kelsi whispered, when it seemed like Bennett was hesitating.

"No, no," he whispered, holding himself above her. His smile was slow and wonderful. "I just want to make sure I remember every second. Every breath."

Their warm skin together felt so soft and so natural. Kelsi arched her back and twined her arms around Bennett.

It was funny how Kelsi had always wondered why something in her didn't want to take this step. She'd thought something was wrong with her. Maybe she was frigid, or dysfunctional.

Now she knew better.

Now she knew that she'd been waiting her whole life for this moment, this boy, this night.

"I love you, Kelsi Tuttle," Bennett whispered.

"I love you, too," she whispered back.

They smiled at each other, and then, just like that, they were no longer virgins.

3

Her first night in Maine, Ella Tuttle tied the ribbons on her platform espadrilles and inhaled the familiar smells of the cottage all around her. It smelled like the beginning of every summer as far back as she could remember: wooden and salty, old and comforting.

What did not smell familiar was the sunporch, where Ella was being forced to sleep this summer. Ella looked around the strange space that she'd never spent too much time in as she got to her feet. This was the guest area in her father's cottage, and aside from making out with Stevie Lewis on the couch once when she was thirteen, Ella had never really paid it much attention. But Kelsi had brought a friend with her this year — Taryn — which meant Ella got to pretend to be okay with being banished from *her* summer bedroom.

Ella might have *appeared* cool with the situation, but the truth was, she missed Kelsi. Kelsi was so wrapped up in her new college life during the year that she'd bailed on family functions and hardly had time to call or e-mail her little sister anymore. Ella had been looking forward to the summer as a chance for her and Kelsi to play catch-up.

At least, the whole extended Tuttle family was in Maine, too, so Ella knew she could turn to Beth or Jamie when Kelsi was off entertaining her friend.

Ella ran through the cottage, waved a good-bye at her dad as he sat with his mystery novel in the armchair by the fireplace, and then burst out through the screen door and into the Maine evening.

"Take it easy!" her dad called, but she ignored him.

She couldn't take it easy — she was too filled up with love.

She loved the pine needles that crunched beneath her totally inappropriate yet undeniably kick-ass wedge heels. She loved the pine trees themselves. She loved the sweet, salt smell of the coming dusk and the not-so-far-off sound of the waves in the bay hitting the sand of the beach. Her family had rented cottages in this small clearing for as long as she could remember. Ella felt as if she'd finally come home, after the long year with all its Catholic school restrictions and annoyances, strict nuns, and dreary detentions. She'd always loved Pebble Beach, but tonight it seemed as if that love had tripled in intensity.

She loved *everything* about Maine, she decided, but especially the fact that her long-distance boyfriend, Jeremy, was now just a few minutes' walk away. Not a couple of hours away in Philadelphia. Not a phone call here or there. Not a text message or a weekend. Just down the road and up the hill. *A few minutes.*

A few minutes that should, Ella felt, begin immediately. She felt that restlessness inside that she'd always thought was just uniquely *her*, but now she knew could be focused.

In this case, on to Jeremy.

She hadn't seen Jeremy since he'd dropped her off at her dad's cottage earlier that afternoon. That was a whole handful of hours they'd been apart, and it was too long. They'd already spoken on the phone twice. Ella loved the little buzz it gave her to know that he was every bit as excited as she was to have the whole summer to enjoy each other — a whole summer without the ticking clock that had been the focus on all those weekends during the school year. It was like the summer was a long, hot bath of Jeremy-time, and Ella couldn't wait to start soaking.

All she had to do was motivate her little posse.

Ella headed toward the picnic tables out on the lawn that served as the central area of the Tuttle family's collection of cottages. Kelsi sat on one of the tables, surrounded by their cousins and the college friend she had brought with her for the summer. Ella enjoyed looking at her family, all together the way they were supposed to be, laughing at some story Kelsi was telling, looking like they all belonged in an Abercrombie ad, only with slightly less bare skin. No one was off at any summer programs this year, Ella noted approvingly. She preferred all the Tuttles present and accounted for, as they were tonight. That was the whole point of Pebble Beach.

Ella took in a lungful of sweet Maine air. How lucky was she that her cousins were her best friends as well as her family?

Ella and tall, toned Beth were the blonde Tuttle cousins, though they looked like two entirely different versions of the "blonde girl" stereotype. They both had long hair, though Ella's was more golden than Beth's and Ella wore hers down around her face in loose curls, while Beth preferred her sporty ponytail. And, apparently, Beth preferred outfits to match that sporty ponytail, despite years of Ella's attempts to trendy her up a little bit. Which, Ella admitted reluctantly, suited Beth's athletic figure best.

What suited Ella was the tight little tank top and short-shorts she was wearing, which she knew accentuated all her curves. It was fun to be a blonde, curvy stereotype, Ella felt, and she had always been about having fun whenever and wherever possible.

Ella's sister, Kelsi, had also been a blonde once upon a time, but had decided to dye her hair a rich, dark brown before going off to college last summer. Now she and her friend Taryn looked sort of alike — both with short, dark hair and intelligent eyes. The similarities didn't stop there. Both Kelsi and Taryn were wearing different versions of the same ratty jeans, flip-flops, and floaty tank tops. Kelsi's was floral with spaghetti straps. Taryn's was a halter top in Kelly green. Ella wasn't sure how much she liked the fact that Taryn and Kelsi looked like peas in their college pod.

Last, but not least, was Jamie, Ella's gypsy cousin, with her dark curly hair, smattering of freckles, and bright green eyes. She was rocking her trademark thrift-store look, with her usual long, belted tunic and a raggedy skirt that showcased her slim legs. Not to mention the roughly seven hundred necklaces hanging around her neck and spilling down her front. Ella suspected Jamie had found the entire outfit for less than five dollars at some garage sale, which she supposed made it even more amazing that Jamie actually looked cute in her secondhand rags.

Ella liked the fact that everyone looked so good, actually. She wasn't one of those girls who liked to hang out with less attractive girls in an attempt to make herself look good. In fact, she thought she got a lot more attention when everyone was equally hot.

"Let's go, ladies!" she commanded, walking up to the little circle and inserting herself into the middle of it. She clapped her hands together like a coach.

"'Let's go'?" echoed Beth. "Are you kidding?" Beth, her smooth athlete's arms bare in the summer evening, laughed up at Ella from her seat on the wooden picnic bench. "You went inside to change all of twelve seconds ago. Literally."

"This is the new, improved Ella," Kelsi told Beth, as if Ella wasn't standing right there. "The one who can get ready for the annual party on the pier in five seconds flat — because she wants to see her boyfriend."

"Cute Jeremy, right?" Beth confirmed. "He was so nice at Thanksgiving. Didn't he bring a casserole?"

"He has *many* talents," Ella bragged with a saucy wink.

"Ella with a long-term boyfriend," Jamie said with a smile, her green eyes dancing. "The mind boggles."

"Boyfriends are overrated," piped in Taryn.

Ella cocked her head to one side.

Taryn smiled at Ella. "Unless he's the right one, of course," she added, possibly remembering that Kelsi also had a boyfriend. Who happened to be Taryn's brother.

Ella chose to interpret that as appeasement on Taryn's part, and therefore decided to be gracious. She smiled back.

"But I still can't believe she got ready that fast, even for Jeremy," Beth continued, shaking her head. "*I* don't even get ready that fast anymore. Did Ella and I switch places? How scary is *that*?"

"We have *not* switched places," Ella told Beth loftily,

and then let out a little sigh, as if she were annoyed. "You are wearing what looks like a Nike running shirt and Gap jeans from, like, six years ago."

"They're not that old!" Beth protested, although Ella noticed she frowned down at her jeans, obviously not sure. "And this is *not* a Nike running shirt!" She paused, considering. "Though I have gone running in it once or twice, now that you mention it."

"Meanwhile," Ella continued, pleased with herself. "I am wearing retro Zara." She indicated her outfit with a little flourish of her hand.

"Can Zara *be* retro? By definition?" Taryn asked Kelsi, who laughed a bit harder than Ella thought was strictly necessary.

"You both look adorable," Jamie said, standing up from the table to link her elbow with Ella's, tugging Beth to her feet with her other hand. "You look exactly like yourselves."

"Thank you," Ella said, because that was exactly what a free spirit like Jamie would say. "Now I would like to hit the pier before it sinks into the bay. If everyone's finished talking about how fast I can change my clothes?"

"Oh, please," Beth teased her. "You love the attention."

"I know," Ella whispered, as everyone got up and started moving in the direction of the dirt road toward town. She gave her cousin a little wink. "But it's fun to pretend."

All the cousins — and Taryn — walked together down the uneven dirt road, through the woods, and then spread out a little bit when they hit pavement on the other side. Ella found herself walking in companionable silence with Jamie, down along the road that ran into town.

They looked at each other and smiled knowingly. Then they both took deep, dizzying breaths the way they had when they were little girls, to suck the summer straight into them. They broke into giggles.

"Are you psyched about Amherst?" Ella asked when she could catch her breath again.

"Yeah, it's been my dream college," Jamie replied, but there was a strange note in her voice. She looked out toward the boats bobbing gently on their moorings in the dark water.

"I remember how much you loved it last summer," Ella mused. "I, personally, find it difficult to imagine that *I* could ever love a *school*, but whatever. You and Kelsi are going to have so much fun, hanging out up there in Northampton."

"It's a terrific place," Jamie agreed, running her hand over the top of a well-pruned bush outside a clapboard cottage.

This time, Ella *knew* Jamie's tone was off. Amherst was all Jamie had talked about since doing that writing program there last summer. Shouldn't she be a little bit more excited? Kelsi had been beside herself when she'd gotten into Smith, and she had never been crazy about that school the way Jamie had always been about Amherst.

Weird, Ella thought.

And then she forgot about Jamie, because they were finally nearing the pier. The entire town of Pebble Beach seemed to be there, reveling in the first big summer party. Ella found herself smiling at nothing in particular, as she breathed in the atmosphere.

Ella could clearly remember other summers. Summers when she'd found the big inaugural party on the pier or the bonfire down on the beach boring. Summers where she'd felt restless and almost needy, like she wanted something thrilling to conjure itself out of seaweed and sand to sweep her away. But this summer she just wanted to embrace all of it. The packs of summer boys with their gleaming eyes and sunkissed skin. She just liked looking at them. The urge to touch didn't seem to be there at all. They were like pretty scenery.

"I'll meet you down by the bonfire," Ella told her cousins.

"Please go find Jeremy," Kelsi said, rolling her eyes. "You're practically jumping up and down."

"Like this?" Ella asked her, jumping up from her toes a few times, mostly so Kelsi — whom Ella totally loved, but who had this whole prudish side to her — could look horrified at the possibility that one of Ella's breasts might fall free of her skimpy tank.

A very high possibility, but then, *Ella* was not a prude. And, clearly, neither was Taryn.

"La Perla, right?" Taryn asked casually, motioning to Ella's pink bra strap under her tank. "Best lingerie in the world."

"Uh, yeah," Ella said, taken aback by the input.

Grinning, Kelsi shook her head. "I knew the two of you were soul mates," she said teasingly to Taryn.

"I should go," Ella said, blowing kisses to her sister, Beth, and Jamie. Then she turned and headed for the spot where she'd arranged to meet Jeremy, trying to brush off the suspicion that Taryn kind of annoyed her.

"Sorry, boys," she singsonged at a deliciously disheveled surfer dude and his completely Chad Michael Murray friend, both of whom grinned at Ella as she passed. "I have a date."

"I could be your date," Chad said with a twinkle in his eye.

"I have a *hot* date," Ella clarified, but with a little smile to take the sting out of it.

Then she forgot the cute surfer boys entirely, bobbing and weaving her way through the crowd. She headed toward the stage where the band was playing something very Death Cab-meets-Sufjan Stevens, but didn't give the band members a second glance — she wouldn't make *that* mistake again. Farther out on the pier, couples huddled together against the wooden railing and groups sat around fishing lines, apart from the madness of the party. Ella made her way to the farthest corner, her pace — and her pulse — quickening as she saw Jeremy standing there, waiting.

When he saw her, a smile flashed across his face and he started toward her, slowly.

He looked so good, Ella couldn't believe it. She felt as if she hadn't seen him in days instead of just hours. He was so deliciously Seth Cohen-ish. That dark hair and sexy, lop-sided grin. His amazing lifeguarding body that he concealed perfectly in baggy jeans and long-sleeved T-shirts. She wanted to eat him up.

They finally reached each other.

"Hey," Jeremy said, and pulled her into his arms.

"Hey to you, too," Ella said back, which made them both laugh a little bit. Ella was usually so forward with guys and the last couple of summers were perfect examples. She had pursued Peter and Ryan with all the confidence in the world. But she couldn't figure out what it was about Jeremy that made her nervous and yet so excited all at once.

"You look so beautiful," Jeremy said, looking down at her. "I mean, you always do, but even more so here."

Ella smirked, ready to snap back with a flirtatious, sarcastic comment.

Until she looked up at Jeremy. He gazed back at her

with his deep brown eyes as if he could never stop looking at her. Ella felt her breath catch in her throat.

Every other guy Ella had been with had obsessed over her looks. Ella had loved it, but part of her had always wondered if that was the only reason they were so interested in the first place. But with Jeremy, she actually *believed* that she was beautiful. And she knew that it was all the more special because he actually cared about her.

Slowly and softly, Jeremy tipped up her chin and leaned in to kiss her. She relaxed for what felt like the first time in days. Jeremy smiled at her softly as he pulled her closer and kissed her again and again, sending a zing of electricity through her body. She slid her arms up around Jeremy's neck, letting her hands run through his messy dark hair, and gave in to the freedom of summer.

No clock, no school, just the two of them and a million stars overhead.

Finally, Ella thought.

Pebble Beach and Jeremy.

She was home.

Beth looped her hair back into a ponytail, and stretched in the lazy morning sunshine that lit up her room in her family's cottage. She took in a few deep breaths — filling herself with the scent of cedar from the chest at the end of the bed. The patchwork quilt on her bed was ragged and perfectly familiar, and Chauncey the cork figurine held his customary position on the shelf above her light switch. Outside, wind chimes made soft murmurs in the breeze, and Beth could smell the fresh kick of the sea wrapped in the scents of woods and earth.

She had been in Maine for two weeks so far. She was happy here. She loved it here.

But something was missing.

Beth headed out into the bright June morning, waving

at her younger cousins, who raced around the grassy central area of the Tuttle compound, playing Capture the Flag. They waved back, but then turned their attention back to their game.

"You have to surrender!" Jessi commanded her brothers, making Beth smile at her bossy tone.

Beth had been something of a loner so far this summer. Kelsi and her college friend were inseparable — constantly making little outings to various places in Pebble Beach, or driving to the outlets in Freeport. They'd invited Beth along, but the few times she'd taken them up on it, she'd felt like a third wheel. The two of them had lived together for a whole year in college, and now spoke in a sort of abbreviated code about their common experiences and friends. Which was mostly funny, but sometimes kind of overwhelming, too. Beth didn't like having to ask for explanations every two minutes.

Jamie, who Beth had imagined would be as interested in finding things to do as Beth was, was instead proving to be hard to pin down this summer. She disappeared for hours at a time, or was always reading. She marked up big books with her pen and copied huge passages in her journal. Beth couldn't tell if she was up to something, or was just relaxing in anticipation of her freshman year at Amherst. She also didn't think Jamie's version of reading looked relaxing — it looked a lot like homework to Beth.

Meanwhile, Ella, who was usually the life of any given party, was completely wrapped up in her lifeguard boyfriend. As far as Beth could tell, Ella spent all day, every day, lounging around the beach, waiting for Jeremy to have time off.

Okay, Beth thought then, heading down the dirt road away from the cottages, that wasn't entirely fair. Ella had spent entire other summers doing exactly the same thing, just *without* the lifeguard boyfriend. Ella simply liked to lie around on the beach, doing as little as possible.

Beth couldn't imagine living that way. It was just one of the reasons she and her cousin were so different. Today, for example, Beth decided to walk over to the local high school so she could work on her times on the track there. She usually just ran in the woods and on the walking trails all around town, but she wanted a change of pace.

It took her about twenty minutes to walk inland across town to the high school. Only the summer people built houses so close to the water, Beth knew. Locals had a much healthier respect for the winter sea, and kept their homes and other important buildings at a distance from the water.

Beth made her way through the bleachers to the track, passing what looked like a summer camp set up on the nearby baseball diamond. Kids were performing calisthenics to the barked commands of a very convincing-sounding drill sergeant. But it was obvious by the way the kids were laughing and having a ball that they loved the guy. Beth had a flashback to some of her favorite times as a kid — at soccer camp with her hard-ass, completely cool, college-age counselors, who were Beth's idols. She could immediately see how much the drill-sergeant guy fit that same image.

Beth grinned to herself, and then scrolled through her iPod playlists to her collection of Training songs, which were differentiated from her Running songs, which were in turn different from her Weight Room songs. She took a couple of breaths as Franz Ferdinand's "The Fallen" began, and then set off running as the drums kicked in.

She was nearing the end of her ninety-minute mix when a baseball bounced onto the track in front of her, then rolled. Beth slowed her run, and pulled her earbuds out of her ears. Any closer and it might have hit her.

She bent over to pick up the baseball, and had a sudden, perfect memory of the years she'd spent playing Little League way back when, in Martin. She wound up, and then threw the ball as far as she could, back in the direction of the base-ball diamond —

And directly over the drill sergeant's head.

Not that he was really a drill sergeant. As he walked closer, Beth could see that he was actually a cute auburn-haired guy maybe a year or so older than she was, who happened to be wearing the same uniform as all those kids.

Beth couldn't help but notice his tight T-shirt that emphasized the long, captivating muscles of his torso, and shorts that rode low on his narrow hips. He was grinning at her.

And to her surprise, Beth found herself grinning back.

"You have a great arm," he said, still smiling. "If I'd known that, I wouldn't have walked all the way over here."

"Thanks," Beth said. Then the strangest thing happened. It was like the spirit of Ella rose within her, and Beth found herself saying almost the same thing her cousin had two weeks ago: "I have *many* talents."

What? Had she really just said that? To this total stranger who might think she was flirting? *Was* she flirting?

"I bet you do," the guy said with another smile. "Unfortunately, I have campers." He looked back over his shoulder, where at least fifteen ten-year-old boys stood at the edge of the baseball diamond, singsonging high-pitched teasing rhymes. He turned back to Beth. "But maybe I'll see you around."

"You never know," Beth said, again as if she were someone else — someone who flirted, someone who enjoyed being flirted with — and he laughed at that, and then jogged back toward his campers.

Beth stuck her earbuds back in her ears and started to run, but she couldn't pretend that her mind was really in it any longer. She couldn't remember the last time she'd even *noticed* a cute guy. It was as if she'd put that part of her life in storage after she and George had broken up last fall. She'd been a boy-free zone for a long time now.

And she'd kind of thought that might be a permanent condition.

But look at her now! Beth felt a little bit giddy, and also impressed with her own boldness. She hadn't had any idea what was going to come out of her mouth.

And the truth was, it felt great.

Because if she was honest with herself, Beth realized as she rounded the track once more, she'd spent a long time getting over George. She didn't regret breaking up with him. But breaking up with him wasn't the same thing as being over him.

Maybe today signaled a new phase in her life, when she'd least expected it.

Maybe she was finally moving on.

Naturally, Beth ran into George exactly four days later.

It was a gorgeous Maine afternoon, with not a cloud in the deep blue sky, and Jamie had actually put her books aside for a change. She and Beth had walked into town together and had lunch down on the beach. They'd gotten hot dogs and waffle fries from their favorite greasy snack vendor, taken their flip-flops off, and walked down to put their toes in the wet sand near the water's edge.

"Wow," Jamie said, swallowing reverently. "I can feel the grease, like, *congealing* inside my body."

"And it's delicious," Beth replied around a mouthful of crispy fries.

"A*mazing*," Jamie agreed happily.

When they were finished stuffing themselves, they washed their hands off in the bay, and then decided to wander around town.

They darted in and out of the cute little shops that dotted the main street of Pebble Beach. Jamie became entranced by some crystals in the New Age store, which, Beth knew from experience, could keep her occupied for hours.

Beth looked out the back door of the shop, to one of the many courtyards that made the town so cute. You could access them from small gates along the main road or from the back doors of the shops, and it was like a whole other layer of Pebble Beach goodness. Across this particular courtyard was one of the village's ice-cream stores, and there was a big commotion outside at the plastic tables.

Intrigued, Beth walked over, and eased her way into the middle of the crowd so she could see what was happening.

Two guys sat at the table, bent over two huge platters of ice cream. Beth knew exactly what they were doing. Every summer, Benny's Ice Cream offered a deal: If you could sit down and eat the entire platter of ice cream — which was like Emack & Bolio's Mack Attack and featured a scoop of every single flavor of ice cream in stock — it was free. But if you didn't finish, you had to pay for the whole thing.

Beth knew all about the contest because George had attempted — and failed — to get his free thirty-seven scoops of ice cream on several occasions.

So really, she shouldn't have been at all surprised when one of the guys lifted his head and she saw that it was her ex-boyfriend-ex-best-friend-ex-everything. She would have recognized George earlier if he hadn't been wearing an out-of-character baseball cap that covered his unmistakably wild hair.

"I am the man!" George shouted to the crowd all around, but mostly to the other guy, who Beth assumed was his friend Dean.

"Ohhh," Dean moaned. "I think I might hurl."

George had done it. He had actually cleared his plate. He had smears of chocolate and strawberry all over his shirt, but his platter was clean. Dean hadn't fared nearly so well: At least ten scoops of ice cream remained, melting sullenly on the platter in front of him.

"I told you not to eat that waffle for breakfast," George told his friend. He whooped. "It's all about pacing."

Beth felt a rush of conflicting emotions. On the one hand, she knew better than anyone how excited George probably was, because he'd been trying to achieve this goal for years. On the other hand, she sort of felt like she was spying on his life. A life she wasn't a part of anymore.

Beth tried to blend back into the little ring of observers, then started for the New Age shop's back door — until she heard her name.

She couldn't exactly make a break for it without looking like an idiot, so she turned around instead.

"Hey!" George looked thrilled. "Did you see what I did? I ate an entire Benny's Big One! Finally!"

"I know," Beth said quietly. "Congratulations." She felt like they were at graduation again.

George rocked back on his heels, and tipped the brim of his cap up, so he could look Beth in the eye.

"You weren't running away in my moment of ice-cream glory, were you?" he asked. "Without even saying hello?" His tone was light, but Beth knew him too well. She could hear the hurt beneath.

"I didn't want to bother you," she said, shrugging.

George shook his head, but his eyes had that glint in them. "Come on," he said. "You alone understand the torturous history of George and Benny's Big One."

"That's true," Beth conceded, and found herself smiling a little bit. "I was there the first time you made the attempt, and bailed after a mere seven scoops."

"I was just a boy, Beth," George said wistfully. "Just a

boy who today became a man." He nodded wisely, and rubbed a hand down along his belly, which had to be killing him. Beth couldn't help laughing.

"Manhood is thirty-seven scoops?" she asked. "Because *I* would have called that insanity."

"Manhood is knowing that thirty-seven scoops are insanity, and figuring out the best strategy for consuming them, anyway," George told her, his eyes dancing with merriment.

"My mistake," Beth said with a sigh, which made him laugh.

"Hey," he said, suddenly serious. "We should hang out some time."

Beth felt her smile slip.

"George . . ."

"In a totally platonic way!" he shook his head at her. His eyes were clear and warm, but nothing more. "Not everybody is as much fun as you, that's all. I drove by the mini golf place the other day, and remembered our hard-core tournaments."

"I haven't played mini golf in a long time," Beth mused, mulling it over. Of course, she should tell George no. There was no point dredging up all that old stuff again. Hadn't she *just started* to feel like she could move on?

But then again, she told herself as George launched into an impassioned description of how he was, in fact, the Tiger

Woods of mini golf, it was *just* mini golf. And maybe the fact that she was starting to move on was why it would be okay to hang out with George. After all, he was still the funniest guy she knew. The funniest *person*, in fact. She missed laughing the way they'd always laughed together.

"Please stop talking," she said, interrupting George's treatise on how his swinging style had developed over the years.

George paused, and bit his lip. "Sorry."

"I think mini golf might be fun," she said, eyeing him with one part hope and another part apprehension. His expression looked the way she imagined hers must: wary, but kind of pleased, too. Because if it wasn't awful, it really would be fun to hang out with George again.

"Yeah?" He nodded. "Um, okay. Cool."

"I guess you should call me," Beth said, feeling awkward. And then she realized that she didn't want to sound like she thought it was a date or anything. "Or I can call you, whatever."

"Sure," George said quickly. He looked at her and smiled that fully George smile. "But we'll definitely do it. It'll be fun."

"Fun," Beth echoed. "I'm looking forward to it."

They smiled at each other, and it was nice, but kind of tentative, too.

"Okay, well, I should go find Jamie," Beth said, beginning to feel awkward.

"Yeah," George agreed. "I think Dean might be in an ice-cream coma."

"See you later." Beth knew she sounded stilted and strange, but didn't know how to change that.

It had never really occurred to her that trying to be friends would be so hard.

Kelsi pushed her way off the subway train, and let the crowd carry her along, up the stairs and out into the sweaty, humid June evening.

Once free of the foot traffic, she backed up to the nearest building, looked all around her, and let the thrill of it all snake through her: She was in New York City!

The plan had been for Bennett to drive up and spend the last two weekends in Pebble Beach. The first weekend he'd cancelled, because his new job at the gallery involved a ton of overtime hours, which he hadn't expected. Then this weekend he'd been supposed to come up again, and when he'd called late last night, Kelsi had steeled herself for yet another cancellation.

"I have to cover all these galleries for Carlos," Bennett had told her. "So I can't come up this weekend."

"It's okay." Kelsi had tried to sound supportive, even though she was crushed. She didn't even know what "covering galleries" meant, or why it was so much more important than his coming up to see her, but she didn't think she should ask that question. She suspected it would sound needy, and she really wanted to sound completely behind him — one hundred percent.

"It's not okay," Bennett replied immediately. "But you should come down. There's no reason why you can't come with me while I do the coverage and, anyway — I want to see you."

And so here she was.

Here being the actual island of Manhattan, which Kelsi could hardly believe she was standing on. She'd been to New York before on various field trips to the Metropolitan Museum or a Broadway show — and even once on an ill-advised night out with Ella — but it had never been like this. She'd never been completely on her own, planning to stay in her boyfriend's *apartment* and cover *art galleries.* Bennett was living in such an amazing world this summer, and now she got to be a part of it, too.

Kelsi pushed away from the wall and started down the street, admiring the sweep of skyscrapers above, and the jam-packed streets spread out in front of her as she headed south. New York was so dramatic, from the eclectic citizens who marched with such purpose, to the bright yellow cabs that zoomed toward certain disaster at top speed only to stop *just* in the nick of time. The sour summer perfume of garbage and hot asphalt rose up from the pavement beneath Kelsi's feet.

Truth be told, Kelsi wasn't sure why anyone would *want* to spend the summer in a place as relentlessly hot and gritty as New York City. She'd foolishly worn flip-flops tonight and could practically feel her feet collecting all the grime and dirt from the hot street. But maybe that was the price for all the restless, exciting energy of the place.

In Maine, the sunset brought lower temperatures. The nights were cool, even cold, and the air was clear. If there *were* stars up above Manhattan, Kelsi couldn't see them past all the bright lights. It was as if Manhattan made its own light, and didn't even need stars. Kelsi laughed a little and turned down the side street that led to Carlos Delgado's gallery.

And Bennett.

At the thought of her boyfriend, Kelsi felt the usual excitement and delight roll through her body. It competed with the clatter and rumble of the city around her, and won, until she was smiling ear to ear.

She didn't really mind that Bennett's job had turned out

to be so much more demanding than he'd anticipated, Kelsi told herself, because he was gaining so much experience and it was going to be such a great thing for his future.

Kelsi realized she could miss Bennett and wish she saw more of him even while totally supporting him. Or, anyway, she felt like she could.

When Kelsi finally reached the gallery, she paused for a moment outside and tried to collect herself. The last time she'd come down, she'd been so excited to see Bennett that she'd burst into the gallery, all sweaty-faced and out of breath. And while no one had made fun of her or anything — at least not to her face — she'd gotten the distinct impression that it *wasn't how they did things in Chelsea.* Bennett liked to joke that all that artistic flair meant a humor deficit.

Kelsi pushed through the big glass doors, careful not to leave any fingerprints because that also *wasn't how they did things,* and wandered into the vast, open space. The gallery spread out in front of her like a labyrinth: white brick walls snaked this way and that, and up above was the balcony where the offices sat.

Bennett had told Kelsi that Carlos was currently showing art and installations related to his concept of summer. That sounded so simple, and yet the art in front of Kelsi was arresting and bold. The canvas nearest her, all cream lines and splashes of blue, made Kelsi gasp a little bit. It was like a perfect depiction of how Kelsi thought a summer afternoon should feel. It was beautiful.

Carlos was amazing. Kelsi knew that. She knew that the art magazines hailed him as the most exciting modern artist of his day. But in that moment, nothing was more exciting to Kelsi than the sound of a voice she knew so well. She wandered past one of the larger installations and watched as Bennett led customers through the labyrinth.

Her heart still somersaulted when she saw him, and she could feel the goofy smile transform her face. It was fun to watch him when he didn't know she was there yet. She could congratulate herself on having such a fine-looking boyfriend, who was dressed all in black today — a tight T-shirt and what looked like new, probably expensive jeans. Even his auburn hair looked different, less emo and more slick. Kelsi remembered Bennett telling her that Carlos had insisted on what he called a "visible upgrade" for his intern. Kelsi couldn't deny that the changes suited Bennett. If it weren't for his trademark hipster glasses, she might have mistaken him for a hot New Yorker.

Until he saw her, that is, and his dark eyes blazed with joy.

Kelsi smiled back, and the nervous tension within her eased. She hadn't even known it was there until she felt it dissolve.

Things were different than she'd expected them to be

this summer, but who cared? The important thing was the look in Bennett's eyes as he walked toward her.

As long as she had that, nothing else mattered.

Bennett's new world was glitzy and wild, and Kelsi loved every moment of it. They'd left Carlos's gallery by taxi, and Bennett informed her that he'd be taking her on an art tour of New York.

"I don't even know what that means," Kelsi confessed.

"No one knows what that means," Bennett replied, holding her close in the backseat of the cab. "But it sounds good, right? You're excited without even knowing why, aren't you?"

"I'm excited." Kelsi nestled close and gave him a long, sweet kiss. "But I know exactly why."

Bennett kissed her back, deeply, and Kelsi had almost forgotten how the sweet pressure of his lips and the familiar touch of his tongue could make her feel. Their arms went around each other, and Kelsi fell back against the cracked vinyl as Bennett trailed kisses down her neck to her collar-bone. She let out a sigh of pleasure, burying her fingers in his hair. She'd never made out in a cab before, and there was something naughty about that thrill, about feeling Bennett's fingers tiptoe up her thigh as the bright lights of New York City flashed by them in a blur.

She and Bennett got so carried away that Kelsi was out of breath and barely noticed that the cab had stopped.

"Crap," Bennett muttered. He handed the driver some bills through the plastic window separating the seats, and then pulled Kelsi out after him.

They were standing in SoHo. Trendy girls in pencil heels wove past them. The front door to a warehouse-like building was thrown open and flashily dressed people milled around within.

"Are you ready?" Bennett asked, looking down at Kelsi with mischief in his dark eyes.

"Of course," she said, fixing her twisted hair.

"Because you're about to see something kind of scary. I call it, the Art Snob." He grinned. "A breed not specific to Manhattan, though this is a major breeding ground. And the one you're about to meet is *particularly* egregious."

Kelsi peered around Bennett, trying to look inside the building.

"Which one?" she asked.

"Me, silly," Bennett chided her. Then he flipped open his cell phone. "This is the most important part of my job. And the most ridiculous."

He pressed a speed-dial button to get Carlos on the line, and led Kelsi into the gallery at the same time.

"It's me," he said into his phone, in a blasé voice Kelsi had never heard before. Then he winked at Kelsi. "No, there's not much of a turnout. Adequate at best."

Kelsi looked around at the crowded space. People were

literally cheek-by-jowl at the bar. Then she looked back at Bennett. Obviously he was speaking in code.

"I mean, sure, there are some people here," Bennett continued. "But we get more foot traffic on a Monday morning at the gallery."

Bennett marched his way through the show, his cell phone planted on his ear, giving Carlos a play-by-play of each piece of art. Kelsi trailed behind, listening.

A beautiful still life?

"Pedestrian," Bennett said into the phone. When Kelsi gaped at him, he pointed at the phone and mouthed, *I love it!*

A painting of a church, with what Kelsi thought was glorious use of light and shadow?

"First-year M.F.A.," Bennett pronounced, while shaking his head at Kelsi, and pointing right at the very shadows that Kelsi had felt drawn to.

And so on, throughout the show.

"Basically, this show is an insult to the rest of the art students," Bennett told his boss as they completed their circuit, despite the fact Kelsi had read in the literature that the artist was self-taught, not an art student at all. "It's everything you complain about," he added. He listened for a few moments and then hung up.

"Wow," Kelsi said, looking at him. "That was quite a performance."

Bennett rolled his eyes. "Did you like it? I hope so,

because we have two other shows to hit tonight, and they'll be exactly the same."

"I loved that church!" Kelsi protested.

"So did I," Bennett said with a shrug. "But it's not about what *we* like. It's about what Carlos would like, and he definitely would *not* like that painting. I have to be his eyes at these shows, not mine. This is what he's paying me for." His eyes twinkled. "Glamorous, huh?"

"That's one word for it," Kelsi replied thoughtfully. "Another one is *weird*."

"Reporting to Carlos is the annoying part," Bennett confided, taking her hand and kissing it quickly, then tugging her along with him to the bar. "But there are compensations."

"Like what?" Kelsi asked.

"Free wine and appetizers, for one," Bennett said, snagging two spring rolls from a passing waiter and offering one to her with flourish. "Or as it's known around here, Friday night dinner."

By the time they finished the report from the third show of the evening, Kelsi was feeling a little bit tipsy from all the free wine — or maybe it was just being with Bennett again. Or being in New York. Whatever it was, when they made their way out of the final gallery onto the busy sidewalk, Kelsi felt a giddy rush all through her body.

"I love you," she told Bennett — and half of Manhattan — grabbing his face between her hands to kiss him.

Kelsi felt as if the kiss could go on forever. Bennett slipped his hands around her waist and lifted her closer to his mouth. They practically breathed each other in.

"I have an amazing idea for our first night in New York," Bennett said, resting his forehead against Kelsi's when they finally pulled apart.

"I think this is an amazing idea already," Kelsi said, kissing him again.

"Trust me," Bennett said softly.

And that was how Kelsi found herself — after a hazardous cab ride through Manhattan that gave her a new appreciation for what a pinball must feel like — in a horse-drawn carriage, being pulled through Central Park at night.

Above, the city lights gleamed like the stars did in Maine, and Kelsi snuggled next to Bennett as the horse clip-clopped through the dark paths of one of the world's most famous parks.

"This is the most beautiful thing in the world," she told him, feeling like she couldn't get close enough.

"No," he said, running his fingers along her face, "you are."

They kissed again and again. Kelsi felt her heart swell, and her skin tingle like she might die if Bennett stopped kissing her. She felt like a goddess. She wanted to collapse into him and never get up again.

Once again, they lost track of where they were and what

they were doing, and only came back to reality when the carriage driver cleared his throat.

From the look on his face as he turned his head, it was not for the first time.

Kelsi giggled, embarrassed, but also secretly excited that she and Bennett could get so involved with each other that even New York City faded away. Bennett had to set his glasses straight on his face, and pretend to be solemn while he paid the driver. They both laughed as they walked away.

Bennett stopped walking, and pulled Kelsi in to kiss her.

"God," he said, "this is crazy. I have to get you home. Like, *now*."

It felt good to be wanted so much, and to want him in the same way. Kelsi moved closer and kissed her way down his neck.

"I'm ready whenever you are," she murmured into his skin.

"That would be immediately," Bennett said, his voice a little bit strained. He stepped into the street and hailed a cab, never looking away from Kelsi or letting go of her hand.

"I'm so glad I'm here." Kelsi looked at him, and the city all around them. "This is all so wonderful."

A cab careened to a screeching halt beside them, and Bennett pulled her close to kiss her one more time.

"It is now," he whispered.

Ella adjusted the top of her black bikini and arranged herself across her towel, making sure her legs appeared to their best advantage. Jeremy was high up in his lifeguard chair, and she knew he'd be watching.

Jeremy had mentioned that he enjoyed glancing down from his ocean-scanning duties to see her there, looking hot. Who was Ella to deny her boyfriend something that required so little effort on her part?

And if the cute-boy parade along the water's edge also happened to notice her as she lounged? Well, that was life. She'd just have to suffer through it.

A wide-shouldered hottie wandered up just then, all square-jawed and curly-haired, and Ella smiled at him, but then saw that his attention was focused on Jamie, who was sitting beside her. As she was very much taken, Ella decided she didn't feel slighted. Jamie had broken up with Dex from her private school way back in, like, February, if Ella remembered right — and she always remembered boys right. Ella had high hopes for Jamie and Mr. Broad Shoulders.

"Hi," he said to Jamie, with a sparkling smile. Ella liked the look of it. "You kind of remind me of Enid from *Ghost World*, which is, like, my favorite movie of all time."

"Hi," was Jamie's response, and she didn't really smile. Ella couldn't believe this was her own flesh and blood, dropping the ball like that. Had she taught Jamie *nothing*?

"I just wanted to tell you that if you feel like playing volleyball, my friends and I are starting a game," the guy continued, still working overtime on the smile. "I mean, volleyball on the beach is definitely more *Baywatch* than *Ghost World*, but I hope you'll give me the benefit of the doubt."

He was adorable. Ella was tempted to go play a little volleyball herself, and she only knew what *Ghost World* was because Jamie had once been obsessed with the movie herself.

Jamie, on the other hand, who had just been told she looked like Thora Birch by a delectable guy, was having none of it.

"Thanks. That's really nice of you," was what Jamie said. She smiled then, but not in any kind of come-hither way. Ella was appalled. "But I'm not really into volleyball. Sorry."

"Um, *hello!*" Ella hissed when the poor guy had taken his glorious shoulders out of earshot. "What just happened?"

"Eh." Jamie shrugged, and dug into her big straw bag for a thick paperback. *Atlas Shrugged*, the cover read. Ella was bored by the very sight of it.

"Not my type," Jamie explained.

"Since when has hot and smart not been your type?" Ella demanded. "Have you gone blind?"

"I don't know, he seemed so *jocky*." Jamie made a face.

"I don't think he was born with that body. He's like Toby Maguire in *Spider-Man*," Ella pointed out. "He may have worked on it a little bit. But then, neither one of us woke up this morning with this hair, did we?"

"I don't know," Jamie murmured.

"Here's what *I* know," Ella said. "The only reason I ever even saw that *Ghost World* movie is because you thought you looked like Enid yourself. Don't think I've forgotten that!"

"Let's just enjoy the beach, okay?" Jamie asked, reaching up to touch her artfully arranged curls as they exploded from her bun. She wrinkled her nose at Ella. "I just kind of want to sit and read my book."

Not an urge Ella shared, but then, she wouldn't have worn the 1950s-looking bathing-suit thing Jamie was wearing, either. It had a *skirt. Different strokes*, she thought.

She closed her eyes and luxuriated in the feel of the Maine sun. It caressed her face and body, and the slight breeze ruffled the hair she'd twisted up in a sleek ponytail. It was a perfect morning, and Ella had the intention of wasting every single moment of it.

"Hello, ladies!" singsonged a familiar voice.

Even before she opened her eyes, Ella knew it was Taryn.

Taryn, sashaying her way through the colorful spread of beach towels, swinging her hips in hope that every single guy in a five-mile radius would sit up and take notice.

Which they all did, because Taryn was sporting a tiny black bikini and nothing else.

The same black bikini that Ella herself was wearing, in fact.

At first Ella thought maybe the bikinis were just similar — after all, a lot of them looked the same. But no. She could see the logo on the hip as Taryn swayed closer, and there was no mistaking it.

It was the exact same bikini.

Ella narrowed her eyes and said nothing as Jamie cheerily welcomed this Single White Interloper into Ella's no-longer-quite-so-perfect morning.

Ella had felt pretty neutral about Taryn's presence up until this moment. Sure, she would have preferred to be sleeping in her traditional place in the bedroom she usually shared with her sister. And yes, it was the teensiest bit annoying that Kelsi always made plans with Taryn and invited Ella only as an afterthought.

But Ella had been handling all that. What she found she was less inclined to handle was someone rolling up in *her* bikini.

Taryn had been lounging around soaking up Ella's dad's attention at breakfast when Ella had announced her plans for the day, and so the other girl had clearly seen what Ella was wearing. Why would she go out of her way to wear the same thing? Ella knew for a fact that Taryn had brought about *seven* other swimsuit combinations to the cottage.

It was outrageous, and, possibly, a deliberate challenge. Ella already had to share her sister's time with this girl. Now she had to share her fashion choices?

The truth was that Ella had never had this issue in Pebble Beach before. Back at school, sure, she and her friend Marilee had been known to tussle a time or two over certain shades of Chanel Glossimer and the odd H&M halter top, but this was Maine. The only other hot girls around, in Ella's opinion, were her family members, and none of them would ever appear in Ella's exact outfits, because they all had such different styles.

Not Taryn, Ella thought then. She took a moment to size the older girl up. She'd kind of avoided doing so previously, in the hopes she could just ignore Taryn's presence in her world. Well, no more.

Taryn was little, like Ella. She didn't have Ella's curves — or her Prada sunglasses, thank you — but she did have the sort of body that called to mind Keira Knightley, the bitch. In fact, she was sort of Keira-d out — from short dark hair to small, cute feet, now that Ella thought of it. Ella, on the other hand, was far more Jessica Simpson.

Taryn plopped herself into the hot sand, and smiled broadly. Jamie smiled back.

"Where's Beth?" Taryn asked.

"She said she wanted to run ten miles today," Jamie replied.

Taryn shuddered. "That sounds incredibly unappealing to me," she said.

Ella could relate, but she hated thinking she had a single thing in common with Taryn.

"That's our Beth," Jamie said with a laugh. "The more exhausting and physical something is, the more she wants to be a pro at it."

"She's the only one in the family who runs," Ella chimed in, clearing her throat. "She has mutant genes, obviously."

"Kelsi runs sometimes," Taryn said. "Never ten miles, though. Kelsi says a couple of miles here and there are good enough."

Ella couldn't believe what she was hearing. As far as she knew, her sister didn't own any shoes that didn't run the risk of being stolen by hippies in a VW van headed for Burning Man. There were no running shoes in Kelsi's closet.

"What are you talking about?" she asked Taryn,

laughing. "The only way Kelsi Tuttle would run anywhere was if someone chased her. With meat, or something. Her vegetarian principles would force her to flee."

Taryn's eyebrows rose over her designer knockoff sunglasses.

"I don't know what her vegetarian principles have to do with anything," she said. "But I do know that Kelsi runs a couple of times a week, usually."

Ella gritted her teeth. It was one thing if Kelsi wanted to take her college roommate everywhere with her like a tote bag. But Kelsi was currently driving back up to Maine from another New York City trip, and Ella didn't see why *she* had to hang out with Taryn in the meantime. *She* didn't need a tote bag.

"So Kelsi should be back soon," Ella said, as if Taryn had asked. But mostly to point out that soon they could get to the bottom of her running habits — assuming she really had any.

"Around three or four this afternoon," Taryn said. Because she knew everything, apparently. "I just got off the phone with her."

"How was her trip?" Jamie asked immediately.

Taryn began to tell Jamie all about Kelsi, because she was clearly an expert on that subject after knowing her for — what? Ten months? Ella had known Kelsi her entire seventeen years. But whatever, that didn't seem to matter much anymore, since Kelsi was now *a runner like Beth*, and who knew what else?

Ella didn't have to check her messages to know perfectly well that Kelsi hadn't called *her only sister*, because Ella's cell phone was located six centimeters from her elbow and it hadn't so much as beeped in the past hour.

It took all the strength in her body not to look at the phone, anyway, of course, and then about twice that strength to keep from biting Taryn's head off. She knew it would only make her look like a gigantic baby.

It was good that Kelsi had a close friend, Ella told herself sternly, even if that friend was a slinky little know-it-all like this Taryn. No, really, Ella knew it was good, and that Kelsi was happier than she'd ever been before.

Ella remembered all the other summers when Kelsi just sort of wafted around in Indian-print batik shirts and claimed to be really interested in the undergrowth out in the forest or butterflies or something, when anyone could see she was actually just sort of lonely. It was *terrific* that she'd found this fun new girl to confide in, and this fun new girl's sort of nerdy brother, for whom Kelsi had unaccountably dumped that hottie Tim, and Ella felt so freaking supportive she practically threw up from it.

"Are you okay, El?" Jamie asked, frowning, and Ella guessed that her "supportive" face needed some work.

"I think Jeremy's shift in the chair is almost up," she said instead of answering. She had to escape. "I'm going to go over there for a while."

"We'll have to hang later, okay?" Taryn said, as if news of Ella's departure distressed her, which Ella very much doubted.

"Absolutely," Ella agreed in the same tone, while getting to her feet.

"Do you mind if I use your towel?" Taryn asked, moving over even as she asked. "I think I forgot mine."

How someone set off for the beach clad in *somebody else's* black bikini, yet somehow neglected to bring anything else along with them, was a mystery to Ella.

"Of course," she said icily, waving at the towel Taryn had already completely taken over. "Be my guest."

"You're a sweetheart," Taryn said in such a way that Ella knew she'd been dismissed.

The *nerve!*

Was this what Kelsi had meant when she'd told Ella that *Taryn and you are so much alike, it's crazy?* Did Kelsi think Ella was a rude bi-atch? That was impossible, of course, since Kelsi obviously didn't think *Taryn* was anything of the sort.

What could Kelsi possibly see in this girl? And what made her think this girl was like Ella? Or — and Ella didn't like this thought at all — did Kelsi prefer Taryn to her own sister? Because Kelsi sure spent a whole lot more time with this person she claimed reminded her so much of her sister than she did with her *actual* sister. Ella's stomach hurt just thinking about it.

But there also wasn't any room left on her towel, so she had no choice but to suck it up and go complain to her boyfriend about Taryn, the Interloping Tote Bag.

7

"I don't know if you know this about me," George said in an overly loud, dramatic voice that attracted the attention of the nicely dressed family of four ahead of them. They were taking, in Beth's opinion, far too much time trying to sink their golf balls into the concrete clown face.

"Why are you yelling?" Beth asked mildly, swinging her mini golf club. She smiled sweetly at the family of four, as if she, too, was baffled by George and his volume.

"I don't know if you know this," George repeated in a fractionally lower voice, "but this past year has stripped me of my charming veneer."

"Yeah?" She started to say *what charming veneer?* but thought better of it. They were trying to be friends, after all.

"At any second, I might unleash the inner demon on that family. I'm just letting you know."

Beth eyed him. "Thanks for the heads-up."

"My pleasure."

Idiot, Beth thought. But it was a fond sort of thought. So far the whole *friends* thing was going okay. It was almost like old, old times.

It was a sunny, breezy summer day — far too beautiful to waste back in the cabins. Beth turned her head so she could see across the mini golf course to the stretch of ocean on the other side of the street.

Beth sometimes wondered what the ridiculous Circus-themed golf course must look like from out in the water, particularly at night when she knew the clown's face, for example, was so hideously lit that it looked creepy and alive. She didn't think she'd ever taken a trip this far up the coast at night. Or maybe she had and had forgotten to look when she was out there enjoying the crisp sea air and the roll of the waves. She wondered if it was possible to see the dancing bears or the truly disturbing clown from out there. The fact that she had no memory of even noticing the mini golf course from the water indicated that probably there was nothing to see. For some reason, Beth found that a little bit depressing.

The family finally vacated the hole, and George stepped into place.

"I'm glad we're not together anymore, Beth," George

announced, smacking his golf ball with a clean, neat stroke and sending it directly into the clown's horrible grinning mouth. It looked like something out of Stephen King. Beth shuddered.

"Because you completely choked on that last hole," George continued with unmistakable glee in his voice, "and as your friend, I can be delighted about it."

"I'm glad we're broken up, too," Beth retorted. "Since we're no longer dating, I don't have to let you win."

George gasped in fake shock, and Beth hid her answering smile. Then she concentrated on making her shot, because she knew she'd never hear the end of it if she didn't.

And also because she was Beth Tuttle and — she could admit it — she hated to lose. She had the usual athlete's approach to any and all competitions. And admitting she had a problem was the first step, she thought with a smirk.

"You have never in your life *let* me do anything!" George was protesting.

Beth tuned him out, a skill she hadn't lost in the months since they'd last spent time together.

And then she made her shot. One stroke. Clean and neat. Perfect.

She whooped with joy and jumped into the air.

"In your face!" she cried at him. "So much for being the Tiger Woods of mini golf!"

"That was luck," George complained. "Total luck. I am way better than you at mini golf. Our entire history proves it. This was luck!"

"Call it whatever you want," Beth said, and let herself swagger a little bit as she headed off the mini golf course toward the new, improved complex, which now included a bowling alley and arcade. For all your Pebble Beach recreational needs.

She was glad George had called a few days ago, and suggested this outing, she thought as she made her way out of the complex. It felt ridiculously easy to be around him. Without consciously meaning to, she felt as if they'd rewound somehow. As if they were good friends again, before all that romantic stuff had come between them and ruined everything.

They wandered out into the parking lot, where the afternoon was lengthening into shadows.

"That was fun," George said. His dark eyes met hers, and he smiled. "You're still fun."

"You, too," Beth said.

By prior arrangement, they'd met at the mini golf course, so there was a small moment of awkwardness as they said good-bye, but then they each headed their separate ways. George took off in his car, and Beth headed through the woods on foot.

Beth stretched her legs as she walked, breathing in the

piney scent of the path in front of her and feeling light, happy. She zipped up her hoodie against the coolness of the shaded woods, shoved her hands into her jean pockets, and smiled to herself.

Her cousins had all counseled her against hanging out with George. They'd warned her that it was a big fantasy to think they could be friends again when they'd once been so much more. Beth had worried they were right, but she'd gone to mini golf, anyway, because she'd wanted to test out their theories for herself. She'd expected it to be a little bit upsetting, and maybe tense, too.

But it had been really good, Beth thought. Who said you couldn't hang out with your first love?

What did her cousins know?

Apparently, more than she did, Beth thought a few days later as she arranged her towel in the sand. Because she'd forgotten that first loves tended to be annoying. Supremely annoying.

Or, anyway, the George variety did.

Had he always been so demanding and weird about where he wanted to sit on the beach? Beth racked her brain, and couldn't come up with a single instance during which he'd ever cared in the slightest.

Which made his theatrics on the beach today all the more irritating.

Possibly he'd done it to impress his friend Dean, whom he'd brought with him today, although Beth couldn't imagine why Dean would find childish tantrums impressive in the least. She threw a dirty look at George.

"Stop giving me that look," George ordered from his sprawled position on the towel next to Beth's, with his huge sunglasses wrapped around the entire upper half of his narrow face.

"You can't see where I'm looking," Beth told him, and snorted. He looked ridiculous and, as far as she could tell, he probably couldn't see at all.

"I can feel it," George retorted. "Like a laser beam to the brain, in fact."

"I just want to make sure you're okay with this spot," Beth shot back. "Are we close enough to the water? Far enough from the trees? Near enough to the lifeguard stand? Far enough from all possible beach irritants, like horseflies and ten-year-old girls?"

"Because you love to sit next to screaming ten-year-old girls yourself?" George argued. "I guess I forgot."

"You're a beach snob," Beth pronounced, almost as if it made her sad. "Have you looked around? Every inch of this beach is gorgeous. You might try appreciating it, instead of freaking out and making us move seventy-five times."

"We moved exactly *one* time," George protested.

"Oh, right, my mistake." Beth looked at him over the

top of her own sunglasses. "The forty minutes we trudged up and down the beach, practically from Portland to Bar Harbor and back again, must have shorted out my brain."

"It would have taken a lot less time if you'd *helped*," George shot back at her. "But no, you thought it would be better to stomp along behind, making snide remarks."

"It's not a snide remark if it's *true*," Beth pointed out. "You were being ridiculous." She paused and cocked her head to one side. "See? Still not snide!"

George's jaw tightened and Beth felt a sudden surge of anger herself. She *wanted* to fight with him, she realized. She *wanted* to be mean.

Which made her wonder if maybe neither one of them was actually mad about the beach.

"Wow," commented Dean, raising himself up from George's other side and looking from Beth to George and then back. It broke the spell, and Beth looked at Dean instead of George, feeling the heat of embarrassment on her cheeks. "Are you sure you're broken up?" Dean added with a grin.

"Yes," Beth snapped, and felt herself blush a little bit when she realized George had said it at exactly the same time, with exactly the same inflection.

We're like Tweedle-dee and Tweedle-dum, she thought sourly. *Even after all this time.*

"Why?" George asked his friend, scowling openly.

"Because you sound like an old married couple," Dean

said in disgust. "I'm going to go jump in the water. The possibility of being sucked out to sea by the undertow sounds way better than listening to the two of you. I feel like I'm hanging out with my parents."

"Great," George said as Dean ran toward the water's edge. "That's just great."

Beth said nothing. Pointedly.

"I don't feel like an old married couple," George continued, sounding aggrieved.

Without even meaning to, Beth snickered.

"I agree," she said when he looked at her. "That definitely had a family feel to it, but more in a sibling sort of way."

"Terrific," George said, sounding peeved. "My ex-girlfriend has become my irritating sister."

"You mean, *my* ex-boyfriend has become *my* annoying brother," Beth retorted.

They looked at each other, and while they weren't smiling, Beth could tell they were both finding the situation funny.

"Ew," George said. "I'm going to swim, too."

"Whatever." Beth pulled her Tess Gerritsen thriller out of her beach bag and cracked it open. "Try not to drown."

"I'll do my best, thanks," George replied, taking off his sunglasses. "And by the way, that sounded like my mother."

Beth watched him walk toward the water, his long, pale

body and that lope of his she knew so well, and let out the laughter she'd been holding in.

Being friends might be tricky sometimes. But family? *That* she knew how to deal with.

This ex thing was going to be a snap.

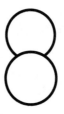

"I'm really sorry, Kels," Bennett told her again. "I just can't leave town this weekend. Carlos is having this big party at the gallery and he's freaking out. I have to stay here and deal with him."

"It's okay," Kelsi said automatically, even though she felt like crying. She pressed the phone closer to her ear. "I just wish I'd known a few days ago. I wouldn't have loaned my car to Jamie."

Kelsi had taken her cell phone back into the bedroom for this call, expecting Bennett to tell her he was on his way. Instead, he'd announced that once again, he wouldn't be able to come up to Pebble Beach. Kelsi would have happily driven down to see him, but Jamie had left a few hours earlier in Kelsi's car to visit some friends down in Boston, and she wasn't coming back until Sunday.

So that meant another long week ahead without the boy she wanted to kiss nonstop.

"Don't be mad," Bennett said into the phone. Kelsi could hear the concern in his voice, and she told herself to get it together.

"I'm not mad," she told him. "Just disappointed."

That was a good word for it, Kelsi thought after they'd said good-bye and hung up. But the truth was, it felt much worse than just *disappointment*. It felt like the air had gone out of the room.

Why did she feel like this? It didn't make any sense. Kelsi knew that things were great with Bennett. She knew he loved her. She knew that he was just busy, and trying to do a good job for Carlos.

But why did her heart hurt?

"What's the matter?" Taryn asked, breezing into the room. She was undressing while moving — flinging her hoodie toward her pile of clothes and stripping her black bikini from her torso.

"Bennett's not coming up," Kelsi said. She didn't bother with trying to modify her tone. "Again."

Taryn gave her a sideways look, and then went and pulled on a T-shirt.

"What?" Kelsi asked.

"I didn't say anything," Taryn replied. "Does he have to work again?"

"Some party," Kelsi said. She could feel herself slumping on the bed. "It seems like Carlos's idea of an assistant is more like a personal slave. I mean, this is Bennett's summer vacation. You'd think he might get a weekend off every now and again."

Kelsi expected Taryn to agree, and thought they might rant about the unfairness of it all for a while. But Taryn was messing around with her hair in the mirror, and she didn't seem particularly inclined toward ranting.

"Well, that sucks for the two of you and your weekends," Taryn said philosophically, "but that's the job."

It felt a lot like a rebuke. Kelsi frowned at her friend, confused.

"I know it's the job," she said.

"Kels, every time I talk to him, he's, like, fully incapable of containing himself," Taryn continued, her eyes meeting Kelsi's in the mirror. "I'm talking full-on joy. He can't stop going on about what an amazing experience he's having. He gets to watch Carlos work — it's beyond Bennett's wildest dreams."

Kelsi looked down. Why was Taryn saying all this like Kelsi didn't know it?

"I understand how cool it is that he has the job," she

murmured, staring at the phone in her hand. She felt very young all of a sudden.

"I'm going out," Taryn said after a moment. When Kelsi looked up, she saw her roommate had pulled on a pair of skinny jeans. "Want to come?"

"Where are you going?" Kelsi asked, trying to pretend her feelings weren't hurt.

"I don't know," Taryn said with a shrug. "I met some guys on the beach earlier. They said there was a party out by some freshwater lake. Are you up for it?"

"Not today," Kelsi said, and summoned a smile. "I think I'm going to take a nap." And if she let herself cry a little bit into her pillow where no one would hear, who would be any the wiser?

"Okay," Taryn said. She walked toward the door, but stopped before walking out. "You know, he really does love this position, Kels. But it doesn't mean he doesn't love you."

"I know," Kelsi said. But she didn't look at Taryn. "I just wish he was coming up this weekend."

Taryn paused there for a moment, and it seemed like she might be about to say something, but then she set her mouth in a line and she walked away.

Leaving Kelsi to feel even worse.

Kelsi spent Friday night moping in her room, and then pretending to be asleep when Taryn staggered in just before dawn. After finally drifting off, Kelsi got up feeling slightly better and wandered into the kitchen. It was lunchtime, and she figured she should eat something. She was surprised to find her sister already there.

"I thought you'd be at the beach," Kelsi said, walking over to inspect the Brie and leftover filet mignon sandwich Ella was making.

"I was," Ella said, wrinkling her tanned little nose. "But then I decided that I needed a Philly cheesesteak for lunch."

Kelsi eyed Ella's plate.

"I think that's more Paris than Philly," she said.

"What can I say?" Ella asked lazily, waving a hand in the air. "I'm so *Vogue* I bring it to my food."

Kelsi smiled at that, and poured herself a glass from the pitcher of sun tea she and Taryn had made the day before. Then she settled herself across the table from Ella, and looked out the window. There were seashells and beach glass on the windowsill to catch the light, and out beyond the open screen, the fresh-cut grass and the woods. Everything was lush and green, with bees humming and the soothing sound of the surf in the distance.

Kelsi just wished she could love her surroundings as much as she had in previous, pre-Bennett summers. Now it was as if she could only see the world through the ache of missing him. It sucked.

"Are you okay?" Ella asked.

Kelsi blinked and turned her attention to her sister. Ella had her hair on the top of her head in a messy yet adorable ponytail, and her brown eyes were filled with concern. Kelsi realized that they hadn't spent as much time together this summer as they normally did — something she'd be surprised Ella even noticed, now that she had a boyfriend.

"I'm fine," Kelsi said.

"You don't look fine," Ella pointed out, licking cheese from her index finger. "You look like someone kicked your puppy."

Kelsi made a face. "I don't have a puppy."

Ella looked at her for a long moment, as if she expected Kelsi to say something.

"What?" Kelsi finally asked.

"You can tell me what's bothering you, you know," Ella said.

But Kelsi couldn't imagine telling Ella that she was this upset over something so incredibly minor. Because she knew it was minor. It was just a cancelled weekend — she and Bennett hadn't broken up or anything. And Kelsi knew that Ella certainly wouldn't mourn a cancelled weekend. In fact, she'd probably take the cancellation as an indication that she should head out and find a replacement.

So Kelsi shrugged.

"It's nothing," she said.

Ella looked down at her plate. "I thought Bennett was coming up this weekend."

"He had to work," Kelsi replied too quickly. She flushed when Ella glanced at her. "Seriously, it's fine."

"Is something going on with you guys?" Ella asked. Her eyes filled with sympathy. "Is it a sex issue, like with Tim?"

"What? No!" Kelsi cried, throwing a hand up as if to ward Ella off. "What are you talking about?"

"You don't have to yell at me," Ella continued, her chin up. "It just seems like the last couple of times you were this upset, it was because of the virgin thing, that's all."

Kelsi gaped at Ella. She hadn't realized until just that minute that she *hadn't* told Ella that she and Bennett had slept together. Her sister still thought she was a virgin. And now that Ella had brought it up, Kelsi wondered if maybe the reason why she was missing Bennett this much was because they'd taken that step, and she felt so much closer to him than she had to anyone else. It was definitely something she hadn't thought about before.

But how could she tell Ella any of this? First she would have to confess that, in fact, she'd lost her virginity. Then she would have to explain that she hadn't meant to keep it a secret. And then she would have to confess to her wild, experienced younger sister — who in her pre-Jeremy days, had gone through boys the same way she went through new ringtones — that Kelsi was all messed up because she'd finally had sex with her boyfriend. She knew exactly how many times she and Bennett had had sex, in fact (four). She was still counting. How could she tell Ella that? Didn't that make her completely lame by default?

So she just shook her head.

"Really," Kelsi said in a low voice, "everything's fine."

Ella's eyes flashed with hurt, and Kelsi reconsidered — but then they both heard the sound of a large vehicle chugging up the dirt road. It was a FedEx truck, which was unusual enough to get both sisters out of their chairs and to the front door.

"Kelsi Tuttle?" the delivery man asked when he climbed down from his high perch behind the wheel.

Kelsi ran across the lawn in her bare feet, flinching a little because the grass was still damp, and signed for the slim package.

"What is it?" Ella asked when Kelsi walked back into the cottage.

"I have no idea," Kelsi said.

She ripped open the package and pulled out a single sheet of eight by eleven paper. On it was a sketch of a girl with short brown hair, lying on her side, asleep.

"Hey," Ella said, delight in her voice. "That's you!"

Kelsi remembered waking up in Bennett's bed the morning after their magical moonlit horse-drawn carriage ride to find him sitting on the floor, sketching her.

You're just so beautiful, he'd told her.

Kelsi opened the card that came with the drawing. It was short and sweet:

I WISH YOU WERE HERE.

And suddenly Kelsi knew that everything really *was* fine. Distance was only miles. Everything else was in her head. She had to figure out how to be okay with what she knew to be true: They were in love. This was just temporary.

Deep in her heart, she believed it.

"Finish your lunch," she told Ella. "I want to go swimming."

The crowd at Ahoy Bar and Grill in town was jumping, as it was every single night of every single summer. Beth stopped on her way back from the bathroom to take a look around the place. She loved that no matter what else might be going on in her life, Ahoy would always have the same rowdy groups spilling out of their booths, shoved in around the bar, and eventually making their moves across the dance floor. It was frantic and loud, and made her feel right at home.

Beth smiled to herself. She'd dressed up a bit, having taken Ella's scathing remarks about her clothes to heart. Of course, her version of "dressed up" just meant a green tank top with tiny little spaghetti straps and a built-in bra.

She figured Ella, who liked to re-create outfits from *Lucky* spreads, still would not approve, but Beth liked the change.

Beth made her way through a cluster of dancing girls, and saw George's familiar head in the booth ahead of her.

Friends could be hard, it was true, but she'd decided a little while after the beach incident that no matter what, she still wanted to try. It didn't seem right that someone who'd meant so much to her could just disappear from her life. George wasn't just an ex, the way girls like Ella had exes in the dozens, interchangeable from one another. He was so much more than just that, for better or worse. He was Beth's childhood, in a lot of ways.

And so what if they occasionally behaved like an old married couple? They had a history.

This was what Beth told her cousins each time someone pointed out that the hang-out-with-the-ex thing sounded like a disaster in the making.

She was eighty-seven percent sure of it herself.

Beth went to slide into the booth across from George, but stopped short at the sight of the female figure already there.

Already there, and laughing merrily at something George had said. It was strange, but Beth could see how he sort of expanded under this other girl's laughter, like a plant under a stream of water. It made her feel sad for him, and for her, too, that they didn't laugh that freely anymore.

But then she shook the feeling off, because George was turning toward her.

"Hey!" he said. "This is Larissa. She fell into our booth."

"It's true," the girl said, grinning up at Beth. "There was a crowd situation and I fell right in."

"But that's not the cool part," George continued quickly. "The cool part is that Larissa's going to Carnegie Mellon in the fall!"

"That's great!" Beth said enthusiastically, although she wasn't sure why.

George rolled his eyes. "My friend Beth is slow on the uptake," he told Larissa. He looked back at Beth as she slid into the booth. "Carnegie Mellon is in Pittsburgh. Pitt is in Pittsburgh. We're going to be in the same city!"

"Have you ever been to Pittsburgh?" Larissa asked George.

"Only for the weekend when I took a tour," George said. "But I'm psyched to explore it. I've spent my entire life in suburban Massachusetts."

"How cool is that Cathedral of Learning?" Larissa asked.

"Pretty cool," George said, looking over at Beth. "It's this huge tower in Pittsburgh."

"Wow," Beth murmured. She was feeling somewhat less at home than she had a few moments before, because she knew absolutely nothing about Pittsburgh. Except the fact that George was going there. And now, Larissa.

"I'm really excited," Larissa continued happily. "I grew up in Rhode Island, and Providence just doesn't compare. Have you heard from your roommate yet?"

"He just e-mailed me the other day," George said. "He sounds cool. What about you?"

"She said she grew up in Pittsburgh, so she could totally give me like an insider's tour," Larissa said. "It should be great, even if we don't end up as good friends."

Beth considered the fact that she had yet to hear from anybody from Georgetown, and wondered if that should worry her. She hoped she wouldn't get stuck with any major partiers, since she had a full courseload and track to keep up with. Not that that was anything new.

Beth looked at George and his new friend, and noticed that they sort of looked alike. Larissa had black curly hair that spilled down her back and big dark eyes just like George. They even laughed alike. She imagined they would make a cute couple, and then waited to see if that thought upset her.

Strangely, it didn't. And *that* made Beth feel a little like crying.

"It's so crazy that we're going to spend a year of our life living with a person we haven't even met yet," George was saying, very animated.

Beth opened her mouth to respond, but then stopped, because it looked like Larissa was getting her first taste of George in his fully excited mode. George ranted about the possible horrors of freshman year, and it was like Beth could see Larissa getting more and more into him every time she laughed. After all, Beth knew the signs. She knew what it felt like to laugh your way into serious trouble with this boy.

And she began to feel all kinds of weird, because as friendly as she and George might be at the moment, and as much as it didn't upset her to *imagine* him with this girl, she wasn't at all sure she wanted to sit there and *watch* as it happened.

"I'm going to go get a soda," she said softly, and it didn't seem like either of them was listening. And why should they pay attention to her, anyway?

Beth pushed through the crowd again, and realized that she didn't feel *jealous.* She didn't necessarily want to hang around watching George hook up or anything, but she didn't want to prevent him from doing so, either.

Beth was dodging a group of people performing the Electric Slide — without benefit of the music — when the truth occurred to her. She'd been concentrating so hard on building a friendship with her ex-boyfriend that she'd somehow failed to notice that her summer was approaching the halfway point. Shouldn't she be meeting people, too? How much could she claim to be moving on when all she did was hang out with George?

"Careful there!" a warm voice cautioned, and Beth felt a strong hand wrap around her bicep and steady her moments before she would have plowed into one of those tiny bar tables.

Beth looked up into a pair of hazel-green eyes. They looked out of a face that was open and friendly, and belonged to a seriously cute guy. He was standing there in khakis and an old, fitted Bruce Lee T-shirt, and he looked thrilled to see her.

"It's you," said the baseball-playing drill sergeant.

Beth shook her head. "Hi. I was a million miles away," she told him.

"Come back to Pebble Beach," he suggested, his grin deepening. "We need you here."

"You don't even know me," Beth pointed out, but his grin was infectious. She couldn't help but grin back.

"That's true," he said. "Although I have a perfect memory of you telling me you had many talents. Besides running, throwing, and looking cute, that is."

Beth felt herself flush with pleasure. It was so girly, and thinking that made her laugh.

"I'm Beth," she said. "Are you a camp counselor?"

"There's a baseball camp just outside of town," he said as he nodded and gently led her a few steps away from the table. "I've been a counselor there for a few years, and went there myself as a camper." His eyes gleamed. "I'm Jimmy, by the way."

"You must really like baseball," Beth said. She remembered the flash of nostalgia she'd had when she'd first seen him at the track. "I used to love it. I played Little League, and on the freshman girls' softball team in high school."

"What position?"

"Shortstop," Beth said, remembering. "It was really fun, but I haven't played since then."

"Why'd you stop?" Jimmy asked. Beth shrugged.

"There were so many other sports I wanted to try," she said. "Swimming, tennis, basketball. Although, between you and me, I'm not as good at basketball as I'd like to be. I'm going to run track at Georgetown in the fall."

"I suck at tennis, but I still like playing, and I love soccer," Jimmy said, leaning closer. "And I play lacrosse on the weekends, but baseball's my first love. My dream is to go out for the majors."

"That would be amazing!" Beth was genuinely impressed.

"We should go for a run sometime," Jimmy said. "There's this cool trail out by my camp. It takes you down so you can see out into the bay from high on the cliffs. It's a great morning run."

Beth grinned at him, and felt her skin tingle. This was the first guy she'd noticed in ages, and here he was, in Ahoy. *And* he was a sports fanatic, just like her. It was crazy.

"I usually go on that inland trail past the swamp," she said, trying to keep the pleasure from showing on her face. "I like the woods a lot."

"We should change it up," Jimmy said with a slow, long look that made Beth feel a little breathless. She loved his confidence. There was no doubt in Jimmy's mind that she was going to go for a run with him.

For a second, Beth wondered if she was ready.

"How about tomorrow morning?" Jimmy offered.

She looked up then, and saw George standing just behind Jimmy, a strange expression on his face.

When Beth caught his eye, he smiled, a little ruefully she thought, and then pointed back toward the table with his eyebrows raised. Larissa was still there, demurely sipping a Coke.

Beth waved him away.

And then felt a little twinge when he went.

This was it. They were both moving on. Right there in Ahoy, on a typical summer evening.

"You know what?" Beth said to Jimmy. "I think I might be in exactly the right mood to change it up. Tomorrow morning sounds great."

George was moving on.

She could, too. Starting right there and then.

Ella hadn't exactly recovered from Kelsi's blowing her off last week. (Her sister had *freaked* when Ella had dared bring up the virginity issue.) Nor was she at all okay about Taryn's continued flaunting of the little black bikini. But after consideration she'd decided to be gracious about all of it. Partly because Ella had decided that Kelsi's refusal to confide in her was just a momentary lapse in sisterly closeness — one that would be fixed the moment they hung out again. But mostly because Kelsi was back from another weekend in New York with her boyfriend and if Ella wanted to hang out with Kelsi, that meant putting up with Taryn the Tote Bag, too.

Easier said than done, of course, but Ella was making the effort.

More effort than she would have thought necessary, since apparently all Kelsi wanted to do with her day was hike to some remote beach (apparently, the one right through the clearing was not good enough) and eat a picnic lunch. Ella didn't understand why a lunch had to be transported across such a distance — it seemed like a whole lot of unnecessary hauling and carrying when the sandwich could be eaten in the comfort of the kitchen in their cottage. But no one had asked for Ella's opinion on the matter.

Naturally, Taryn had been absolutely thrilled with Kelsi's long-distance picnic prospect, and the two of them had been busy making their lunches when Ella discovered them in the kitchen that morning.

It did not escape Ella's notice that the two girls were not planning to invite her along.

It seemed that now she had to wait to be *invited* to spend time with her *only sister*.

"Cool," she'd said when they'd explained what they were doing. "I think I'll come, too."

The looks Taryn and Kelsi exchanged at that point were just plain obnoxious, but Ella had ignored them. There was no point getting mad if she wanted to be included in their plans.

She would just have to ignore the part of her that was pissed that Kelsi would try to exclude her in the first place.

"I don't think hiking's really your thing, El," Kelsi had said gently, which was worse than if she'd just said no.

Meanwhile, Taryn made herself look very busy with the sandwiches. Overly busy. Ella actually hated her for a moment. Because there was no question about whether *Taryn* would be invited along. After all, Kelsi loved Taryn so much that Ella had been relegated to the pullout couch on the sunporch for the summer, instead of the bedroom she'd shared with Kelsi for their entire lives. Ella hadn't even complained about it, and now this? It was so unfair.

"Don't be ridiculous," Ella had announced breezily. "I *love* hiking!"

There was no mistaking the expression on Kelsi's face. Ella had seen it many times before. It was the face Kelsi wore when their smaller cousins demanded she take them somewhere she would have preferred to go alone. It was half-suffering, half-patronizing, and Taryn's answering shrug was just as bad.

They were *tolerating* her.

It was hideous.

Which was how she'd come to find herself scrabbling her way down a rocky cliff while Taryn bounded alongside Kelsi like some kind of freakish mountain goat. But if this was what it took to reclaim Kelsi, then Ella would do it.

Assuming she didn't fall to a bloody death on the rocks below, that was.

Down at the bottom of the cliff, there was a perfect, pristine little cove that Ella had never seen before. It was like something out of a movie. One involving Leonardo DiCaprio back when he was young and cute. Ella missed those days.

"This is just beautiful," Ella said with an appreciative sigh, smiling at her sister. She was tempted to reconsider her lifelong position on hiking, that's how gorgeous the little cove was.

"I know," Kelsi said, smiling back, and for a moment everything seemed normal and okay. "Tim brought me here last summer."

Ella breathed a little sigh of remembrance for Hot Frat Boy Tim (as she always thought of him), Kelsi's ex, whom Ella had found very amusing on an otherwise not at all fun road trip last summer. As she stared at the rocks and the clear water breaking over them, she also remembered the awful fight she'd had with Kelsi by the side of the highway later, during that same road trip. She thought about how angry Kelsi had been, but how she'd chosen to forgive Ella for sleeping with her boyfriend Peter the summer before.

Well. Technically, Kelsi and Peter had been broken up when Ella had slept with him. Yes, only for a few hours. But still, broken up.

Anyway, Ella still felt awfully guilty about the Peter betrayal, and forever grateful that Kelsi understood how badly Ella felt. Thinking about all of that history reminded Ella of how much she loved her sister, who had decided to overlook something most people wouldn't.

"The cove was like this magical escape then, too, right when I needed it," Kelsi was saying, still gazing around.

"Ah," Taryn said significantly, and then looked over at Ella.

Which was when Ella realized that Kelsi had told this total stranger about the sisters' big fight the summer before, in all its detail. It made her feel like throwing up. Fury shot through Ella.

But she didn't know what to do about it.

"I'm hungry," she announced carelessly, like she hadn't gotten Taryn's point. There was another shared look between Taryn and Kelsi, but Ella figured that was better than exploring the previous subject.

Ella searched around in her knapsack, blinking back the heat that surged behind her eyes, and pulled out the turkey sandwich she'd thrown together in the fifty seconds she'd had to get ready. She took a huge, angry bite and pretended it was Taryn's head.

"Oh," Taryn said, looking at Ella. "Do you still eat meat? I don't know why I thought you were a vegetarian."

Ella didn't know why, either. The Tote Bag had, by this point in the summer, had so many meals with Ella during which Ella indulged her inner carnivore that Taryn would have had to *deliberately* not notice it.

"Kelsi's the vegetarian, not me," Ella replied, forcing a smile. *Duh*, she thought. *I'm eating turkey, aren't I?*

"Kelsi's actually vegan," Taryn said, because, of course, she knew everything about Kelsi. "We all went to this PETA rally up at school this winter, and it changed us. Probably for good."

"You're vegan?" Ella demanded of her sister, ignoring the whole PETA aside, because she was tired of all of Taryn's little stories about how she and Kelsi were so much like sisters, or maybe identical twins.

"I'm trying," Kelsi said, smiling back at her, but kind of quizzically. "Why? Since when do you care what I eat?"

"I really don't," Ella said, and took another bite. Which was true. She didn't care what Kelsi ate. What she cared about was the fact Kelsi no longer shared anything with her.

Kelsi and Taryn launched into a discussion of their mutual friends, none of whom Ella knew, and so she just ate her sandwich and felt like a bratty little kid. An *unwanted* bratty little kid, which was even worse.

She was stuck at the bottom of a cliff, she was miserable, and it was perfectly clear to Ella that Taryn had completely usurped her position in her sister's life.

"I just don't know what to do about it," she complained to Jeremy a few nights later.

Ella's legs were still protesting from hiking the other day, or possibly from her selection of extremely precarious cork wedges. She wished they didn't have to walk all the way back from the old movie theater that was Jeremy's second home in Pebble Beach. But there had been a John Hughes eighties movie marathon, and they'd obviously had to go. Eighties movies remained Jeremy's greatest passion. Other than Ella, that is.

"Why do you have to do anything?" Jeremy asked in his reasonable voice. "Sometimes you don't feel all that close to Kelsi, either. So who cares if she feels closer to Taryn right now?"

It was his *overly* reasonable voice, actually. It was the one he used when he thought Ella was being *un*reasonable.

"She's essentially stolen my sister!" Ella cried. "I have to do *something*!"

"She's your sister," Jeremy pointed out calmly. "She's always going to be your sister. It doesn't matter if she has other friends."

But it mattered to Ella. It mattered that Kelsi thought Taryn was so wild and untamed and fun, which were the ways she *used* to describe Ella. It mattered that the other friend in question was basically a different version of Ella, but one — and this hurt to admit even to herself — that Kelsi clearly liked better.

Ella curled her hand tighter into Jeremy's, and leaned into him as they walked back into town.

It was another beautiful summer night, with a great mess of stars above, and people milling around in the quiet village streets. Music echoed off the water out in the bay, and laughter hung in the air like fog. The night felt thick and secret all around them, and Ella loved that the temperature had dropped enough so that she could feel cozy in her hoodie, with Jeremy right next to her, giving off heat like a furnace.

If there was a better place than Pebble Beach, Ella didn't know what it was. She reached up and pulled Jeremy's head closer to hers, so she could kiss him with all the sweetness she felt in the summer air around them.

He held her close, and the kiss changed. It got hotter, and Ella moved closer, pressing herself against him to hear his sexy little groan, until they remembered where they were.

"Oops," Jeremy said with that lopsided grin Ella adored. He swiftly kissed her once more, then took her hand and kept walking.

Together, they wandered down Main Street, skirting the lines outside Ahoy and the Lighthouse. Ella had wanted to go out, but now, after that kiss, she was far more interested in returning to Jeremy's place, where he basically had the house to himself. She could tell from the longing look in Jeremy's eyes that he felt the same.

They were walking past the big group of bars and shops when Ella happened to glance over at a couple sitting on a bench near the little Chamber of Commerce shack. She didn't know what caught her eye. Maybe it was the way the guy held himself with easy confidence that made him seem like a better person than she knew him to be.

But Ella thought that really, she'd noticed the girl. She was wearing a beat-up pair of Bermudas and a breathtakingly daring halter top, and she looked even more like Keira Knightley than usual.

Taryn. The Tote Bag.

And the guy she was making time with was none other than Peter.

Peter, who had broken Kelsi's heart by sleeping with another girl three seconds after she'd dumped him.

That other girl being Ella herself.

All that pain and upset because of one midnight-eyed guy with smooth shoulders and a wicked grin, and Taryn was touching his arm and leaning in close like she didn't know anything about it.

Except she did. Ella knew she did.

Ella felt a surge of rage, and something like triumph, too. It was dizzying and made her breathless.

If Kelsi had been upset about Ella getting with Peter, *this* was going to kill her.

Ella didn't know if she wanted to race home and expose Taryn's behavior to Kelsi immediately, or just run over to the bench right now and have it out with Taryn on Kelsi's behalf.

Not to mention that she could think of a few things to say

to Peter, too. Like, why had he texted her all last summer? After completely failing to call her the summer before?

Her stomach churned. Her head spun.

"What is it?" Jeremy asked, and Ella realized they'd stopped walking. Ella tugged his arm, and led him away from the scene of the crime before she knew what she wanted to do. "Is something wrong?" he asked, frowning down at her.

"Everything's fine," Ella lied, because she needed time to think. To plan out what she should do.

"Are you sure?" Jeremy asked. "You look kind of weird all of a sudden."

"I'm fine," Ella said.

She forced a smile, and eased her body against his to remind her of all that heat she'd been so excited to play with just a few moments before. It worked, too. Touching Jeremy always made everything better, and it gave her time to think.

"Come on," Jeremy said then, holding her face with his hand. "I can think of better things to do than stand out here in the street."

"That depends on what you're doing while you're standing in the street," Ella teased him.

She would think about Taryn and Peter tomorrow, she thought as her boyfriend gave her a wicked grin, and led her toward his house.

Tomorrow she'd form a plan.

It was hard, Kelsi thought, stripping off her bathing suit and rummaging around for something dry to throw on. Her family was gearing up for one of their trademark barbecues, and all she felt like doing was curling up in a ball, missing Bennett, and sulking.

She missed him all the time. She missed his warm, easy presence when she woke up in the morning, and she missed the warmth of his hands on her skin. She missed him every time Taryn told her she was moping, which was about seven times a day. She missed him every time she wanted to tell him something, and had to decide whether it was worth bothering him at work to do so.

Kelsi had never been the clingy type. It was just that during the school year, she and Bennett had spent every possible second together. It felt so bizarre to be cut off from him now. At least it was just for the summer. Kelsi was practically counting the days until school started again, and things returned to the way they were supposed to be.

Checking the clock on the table between the two twin beds, Kelsi saw that it was six thirty P.M., and Bennett should be wrapping things up at the gallery. He usually had an hour or so to himself before Carlos's various nighttime activities began. Quickly, she pulled out her phone and pressed his number.

"I'm so glad you called," he said instead of a hello. His voice was warm and brimming with laughter. "You won't believe what just happened."

"Tell me," Kelsi said, smiling. She lay down on her bed and let his voice flow over her.

"This horrible old woman came in, and was going on about the art she wanted to put on her wall. She wandered all over the gallery, and complained because — and I'm not exaggerating — she didn't understand why Carlos couldn't paint something *pretty*." Bennett laughed. "Can you imagine?"

"That blue-and-cream piece in the entryway is pretty," Kelsi said, trying to catalog in her head the different canvasses Bennett had shown her. They weren't all experimental or particularly daring. Some of them really *were* pretty.

"Carlos's work is a lot of things," Bennett replied

impatiently. "Important, maybe. Or evocative. But *pretty*? Please. She can go to Bed, Bath & Beyond and get a Monet water-lily print."

Kelsi let that comment sit there for a moment. She felt kind of hurt, and she wasn't sure why. It had something to do with that tone Bennett had used. Like she was as *pedestrian* as the still life he had described to Carlos over the phone.

"I just called to say hi," she said eventually. "I was missing you."

"I miss you, too," Bennett said, back to his normal, sweet tone, but Kelsi still felt off-balance.

When she hung up a few minutes later — Bennett had a dinner party to attend and had to run — she felt a good deal more unsettled than she wanted to admit. She wondered if Bennett's Art Snob persona maybe wasn't such a joke to him anymore.

Shaking it off — because she could smell the grill firing up — she pulled on a pair of jeans and a high school sweatshirt, and headed outside into the cool evening.

Various Tuttles roamed around the grassy area in the center of the cottages as dusk fell all around them. The littler cousins chased lightning bugs in and out of the darkening woods, the aunts sat and sipped wine and ate cheese from a round wooden platter, while Kelsi's dad was busily flipping burgers and telling lies to Kelsi's uncles about his latest deep-sea fishing trip.

It was a perfect family scene, and Kelsi knew that she should enjoy being a part of it, but instead, she found herself feeling sort of empty. She wondered if it was the phone conversation — as if maybe she knew, deep down, that things with Bennett were changing.

Or maybe, she thought with a rueful smile at her own drama, she was just having a blood-sugar crash, and should get some dinner.

After coaxing her father to grill her a veggie burger, Kelsi headed toward the picnic tables. At one, Ella and Jeremy were talking animatedly with Beth, George, and a freckled, athletic-looking boy whom Kelsi didn't recognize. Kelsi smiled at them as she passed, and then sat down at the next table with Jamie and Taryn.

"I know I've been in my own world since I got back from my last New York trip," she said by way of a greeting, "but I'm pretty sure I've never seen that guy before. Have I?"

"His name is Jimmy, and he's Beth's new person," Jamie explained, her green eyes dancing. "Apparently, they've been running in the mornings, which is like flowers and dinner dates in *Beth's* world." She leaned in close. "And George is here as an honorary Tuttle, thanks to Beth's dad, who ran into him yesterday. Except Beth said that he's not pining or anything because he met some chick who's also going to school in Pittsburgh this fall, who seems nice, who she thinks he might be dating. Beth and George are moving on *together*, it seems."

Finished with that involved summary, Jamie proudly sat back and popped a carrot into her mouth. Kelsi looked over to the other table.

Ella and Jeremy looked to be in high spirits, as Ella told some tale to Beth's new guy, one that involved lots of hand gestures. But the new guy kept glancing over at Beth and George. They were talking to each other, with George tapping out points on the wooden table, like he was either drumming or giving a presentation.

"Yikes," Kelsi murmured.

"Exactly," Taryn agreed, snorting with laughter. The only other person who snorted when she laughed was Ella, Kelsi thought, which made her love the both of them even more.

"Maybe not *yikes*, exactly," Jamie said, frowning slightly. She shrugged. "I've always loved George. I think it's really cool that they're trying so hard to be friends."

"Has that ever worked, though?" Kelsi asked. She remembered how insanely in love George and Beth had been, and how badly they'd hurt each other. "In, like, all of human history?"

"I can't even watch," Taryn told Kelsi. "It makes my head hurt."

Kelsi tore her gaze away from what she was certain was the impending catastrophe at the next table, and focused on Jamie instead.

"I'm so excited that you're going to Amherst!" Kelsi told

her cousin. "Bennett's already promised to give you the full rundown on campus life. Taryn and I are always there, and we'll get to hang out all the time. Next year is going to be amazing!"

"I love Northampton," Taryn chimed in. "It's this totally crunchy but hip little town, with zillions of bookstores and thrift shops and cafés. It's such a great place to live. You'll definitely love it."

But Kelsi noticed Jamie didn't respond. "I'm so hungry," she said eventually. "I'm going to go grab some more of my mom's Caesar salad. Do either of you want anything?"

Neither one of them did, because they were both stunned and staring at her, so Jamie got up and hurried away.

"Um, that was weird, right?" Taryn asked when Jamie was out of earshot. "She totally didn't want to talk about school. I figured she'd be so excited about Northampton that she'd consider transferring to Smith, to be honest."

"Yeah . . ." Kelsi frowned after her cousin. "I don't know what's up with her. She's the most driven one of all of the cousins. She usually can't shut up about how great Amherst is and how psyched she is to be going there."

"Maybe she's freaking out," Taryn said with a shrug. "Remember how scared we were at the beginning of the year?" What Kelsi remembered was that *she* had felt terrified, while Taryn had seemed in her element, but she opted not to say anything.

"Yeah, but Jamie spent all last summer there," Kelsi said instead. "There's no fear of the unknown — she's already done it!"

"Then, clearly, she's just weird," Taryn concluded with a wink, making them both crack up.

The night darkened around them, and they lit citronella candles in the center of the picnic table to keep the mosquitoes at bay. Kelsi loved the tangy smell of the candles, and she stared into the center of the flame, while above them the night sky was a dark blue fading to black.

"Did you talk to Bennett today?" Kelsi asked Taryn when they were picking at fresh berries and debating about making vegan s'mores over the fire.

Taryn shook her head. "He's always so busy," she said. "Running around for that guy. Why, what's up?"

"Nothing." Kelsi sighed. "I don't know. Sometimes I feel like maybe New York isn't the best thing that ever happened to him, after all."

Taryn frowned. She looked impatient for a moment or maybe Kelsi just imagined it, because her face cleared.

"Are you kidding?" she asked. "Maybe he didn't tell you this, but he's been obsessed with Carlos Delgado since he was, like, nine. I mean, total hero worship. This is a fantasy come true for him."

"I know, and I think it's amazing for his career *and* his art," Kelsi said quickly.

"This is his dream, Kelsi," Taryn said. She looked confused, and taken aback. "I thought you understood that."

"I do," Kelsi said, feeling like the conversation had completely gotten away from her. "That's not what I meant at all."

But she didn't know how to explain what she meant. She didn't know how to talk about her boyfriend to her best friend, when the boyfriend in question was her best friend's brother, and Taryn was clearly feeling protective. And Kelsi knew why: Taryn had confided that she had spent years running interference with high school girlfriends of Bennett's who had tried to get to him through her. Kelsi understood.

But it made her feel so alone.

Taryn decided to get the stuff to make s'mores then, and Kelsi sat solo at the picnic table, inhaling citronella fumes and mentally kicking herself.

How was Taryn supposed to respond? Bennett was her brother. The fact that she and Kelsi were best friends just made moments like this incredibly awkward.

Because while Kelsi knew what a huge opportunity working with Carlos was for Bennett, she wasn't sure it was the best thing for *him*. Like, for his *character*. Tonight wasn't the first time she'd thought he was becoming kind of snobbish about art. She would have thought that the generous, enthusiastic guy she knew so well would have welcomed the opportunity to find *something pretty* for a nice old lady, instead of mocking her.

Her phone vibrated in her pocket, and she pulled it out. It was a text message from Bennett:

SORRY, BAD DAY, LOVE U.

And just like that, Kelsi's entire mood lifted.

How pathetic, she thought. She should be ashamed of herself for being such a *girl.* But she couldn't deny the flush of happiness that washed through her, altering the whole night around her. She couldn't deny that just hearing from him when she didn't expect to made everything seem better. So what if it was pathetic — it was also true.

She vowed to be more supportive and less judgmental.

It was only a summer, after all.

Only a summer, Kelsi thought, *and it's halfway over already.*

"You better save me some marshmallows!" she called across the clearing to Taryn, and found she was all but skipping as she got up and headed toward her friend.

The first step was to make sure that what she thought was happening was really happening, Ella told herself. There was no point doing anything until she was sure.

After all, Peter was beautiful and smoldering, and he could lure any unsuspecting girl into his little web. Ella knew this better than anyone. It wasn't so hard to imagine a scenario in which Taryn accidentally got involved with a hot guy one evening, only to discover later that it was *the* hot guy who'd treated Kelsi so badly way back when. In this imagined scenario, Ella found she could give Taryn the benefit of the doubt.

But she knew that was only because she didn't believe it.

Taryn knew exactly who and what Peter was. Ella was certain of that.

And because Ella was certain, she wanted to be extra careful in proving it. Because she could tell that Kelsi wasn't going to accept the ugly truth about her supposed best friend without a boatload of evidence.

This was how Ella convinced herself that her only option that Friday night was to follow Taryn.

Kelsi had gone down to New York again, a last-minute trip brought on because Bennett had to cancel coming up once again. Ella didn't think it was too cool that he kept doing that to Kelsi. She happened to be an expert on the long-distance thing, having first failed at it, and then succeeded at it, all during this past year. With the same person, in fact. One thing she knew: You had to make time for the other person or you could forget about it.

But Kelsi's long-distance relationship wasn't really what was occupying her thoughts tonight.

She was determined that tonight she'd figure out what was really going on between Taryn and Peter.

Ella lounged around in the living room in her old Juicy sweats, yawning and reading *Allure*, looking like she planned to spend the night in. She waited until Taryn got the inevitable call on her cell phone. When Taryn started whispering and giggling, and then took the call to the bedroom, Ella moved herself to the sunporch and changed into something more appropriate for going out — in this case, a denim miniskirt, layered tank tops, and ropes of long beads.

It wasn't that hard to slip out of the cottage and wait in the shadows by the side of the dirt road. By this point in the summer, Ella knew the whole stretch of that road like the contents of her closet. She could walk it with her eyes closed, which was a good thing, as it was usually far too dark to see anything, anyway.

Soon enough, Ella's eyes adjusted enough so that when Taryn walked past, she could see her — or enough of her, anyway. Ella would know that saucy little walk anywhere, it annoyed her so much. It was easy enough to follow Taryn, keeping to the shadows and trailing her all the way into town. Ella was grateful her cork-soled wedges were silent on the pebbles.

Once in the village, there were other people around and Ella was able to draw closer to her prey. Taryn was dressed for a party. Her jeans were supertight and low, and her black tube top bared most of her abdomen and all of her shoulders. It was the sort of outfit that *should* have looked cheap and, Ella noted sourly, didn't look anything but hot on Taryn.

It just made Ella all the more determined to bring her down.

Taryn walked with confidence up to the Lighthouse, the new-ish bar in town that Ella had so far been completely unable to do more than peer into.

Ella waited for the gigantic bouncers to do their job, and deny entry to underage Taryn, but she just flashed an ID and sauntered right in.

Ella gritted her teeth. *Ugh.* It had never occurred to her to get a fake ID. She'd always relied on her charm and the kindness of well-positioned boys.

Ella knew the bouncers were a lost cause, having tried to talk her way past them last summer, so she looked around for other possibilities. It didn't take long. Around the back of the bar, a guy who looked like a bartender stood next to the propped-open back door, smoking a cigarette. It helped that he was cute, but it didn't actually matter.

Ella smiled, and made her move.

"Hey there," she singsonged, swaying her hips as she walked over to him. "What's going on?"

"Smoke break," the guy said, and then looked surprised, like he hadn't meant to say something so obvious.

Ella smiled wider.

"What do you want?" he asked in a gruffer tone, clearly trying to be all tough.

"I want to go inside," she said, cocking her head to the side. "I want you to let me in."

He smiled back, as if against his will.

"Now why would I do that?" he asked.

"Because you like me," Ella suggested, encouraging him to agree with the jut of one hip.

"And what's in it for me?" he asked after a long moment. But Ella knew she already had him. It was right there in the smile he was trying to hide.

She let her hips roll as she sauntered to the open door, and pulled it open. She stepped close to him, but not too close, and looked up at him through her lashes.

"If you're nice," she told him in a low voice, "I'll let you buy me a drink."

And then, before he could react, she stepped inside.

Ella was feeling pretty good about herself as she navigated the forbidden zone of the Lighthouse. She figured she probably wouldn't be back any time soon, so she took a small detour from her Taryn surveillance to check the place out. It was all plush red booths and dark decor, and it made Ella feel like an adult just to be inside. She liked the big, modernist paintings on the walls and the funky music from a DJ spinning in the corner that filled the place with a sexy, underground vibe.

But she could only revel for so long before her mind returned to the purpose of her visit: the treacherous Taryn.

Carefully, Ella made her way through the maze of booths,

making sure that her face stayed largely obscured behind a group of girls here or a big guy there. It helped that the bar was so dark and smoky. Eventually, she found what she was looking for.

Taryn and the horrible — though, tragically, still freaking hot — Peter were sitting entirely too close together in one of the booths near the door. As she glared at them, Ella realized that her stealth was unnecessary, since Taryn hadn't once looked away from Peter's face.

Ella remembered exactly how mesmerizing he could be. Those dark, dark eyes and that cocky smile.

Ella couldn't believe that Taryn would do this to Kelsi. Ella's outrage simmered near a boil, but she held it in, and simply watched from behind a pillar.

They had a drink. They kept touching each other. They laughed and laughed. Eventually, Peter's hand disappeared beneath the table, and it didn't take a lot of imagination to work out where it went. Ella knew exactly what that felt like. She could see those feelings she remembered on Taryn's face. It was crazy that she was standing here, watching this happen.

Soon after, the happy couple threw some money on the table and headed for the door, with Ella not far behind. They never glanced around. Once outside, they started down the street. Ella danced around the bouncers — hoping they didn't get too close a look at her — and followed.

About halfway down the street, Peter stopped walking, and pulled Taryn up against the side of a building, at the mouth of an alley. They started kissing, fiercely. They were plastered together. It was hot, and it should have been private. Ella didn't know whether to stare, scream, or run away.

Taryn's hands were all over him. His hands were all over her skin, everywhere the flimsy tube top wasn't. He yanked her up against him and she wrapped her legs around his waist, and still, they didn't stop kissing.

It was only when they retreated farther into the shadows of the alley that Ella forced herself to turn and run away.

The next day, Ella spent the morning with her cousins on the beach, sunning herself, reading *Vogue*, and fuming.

Taryn joined the group just before lunch, looking sleepy and not at all guilty or ashamed.

Ella had to work overtime not to throw her magazine at Taryn's head. It was the extra-heavy fall issue, after all, and it might have knocked her out.

"Okay," Jeremy said, appearing in front of them. "Who's up for lunch?"

Ella smiled up at him, and let him pull her to her feet. She also let him kiss her a little bit — but not much; she had important things on her mind.

"Let's go to the Snack Shack," Beth said, naming the

deliciously greasy snack bar steps from the beach. "I want a big cheeseburger."

The group headed off to lunch together. Ella laced her fingers with Jeremy's, and liked the way he squeezed her hand.

"Are you having fun even though Kelsi's not here?" Beth asked Taryn as they walked.

Ella wondered how concerned Beth would be about Taryn if Beth knew what Taryn was really like. She remembered how cruelly Beth had treated Ella herself in similar circumstances, and pursed her lips.

"Oh, sure," Taryn said easily. "I'm pretty good at entertaining myself."

"Like last night," Ella said, as if agreeing.

Taryn looked at her. Always interested in something gossipy, Ella's cousins all but perked their ears.

"What happened last night?" Jamie asked, clearly thrilled at the possibility that something scandalous might have occurred. It was the writer in her, Ella knew. She always wanted the story.

"Oh, *I* don't know," Ella said casually. She looked at Taryn. "Didn't you go out?"

"Yeah," Taryn said, blinking. "I did. This place called the Lighthouse?"

"That new place," Beth said, nodding. "They have a

tough door policy. I can't get anywhere near it, unless I want to go there for lunch. And I think all they have then is clam chowder."

The conversation looked as if it was going to turn into a debate on door policies and New England clam chowder. Ella couldn't have that.

"Did you go by yourself?" she asked Taryn, with all the feigned innocence in the world.

Taryn looked at Ella again, like she could sense that Ella was after something but wasn't sure what.

But Ella knew that Taryn knew perfectly well what Ella was after.

"Actually, no," Taryn said slowly. "I kind of met this guy the other day."

"Met" was one way to put it, Ella thought.

"Tell us everything!" Jamie demanded, her green eyes sparkling.

"Not much to tell," Taryn said, and Ella had to suppress a snort. "Just a guy. He's cute, and kind of funny . . ."

So, Ella thought darkly. *That makes it okay to screw over Kelsi, is that it?*

"Do we know him?" Ella asked pointedly, trying to sound as if she was just casually interested. "Is he a summer guy or a townie?"

"He's just a guy," Taryn said again, her eyes meeting

Ella's, hard. Then she shook her head. "I'm going to run to the bathroom. I'll meet you guys over in the food line."

Because they didn't know enough to dig deeper, Beth and Jamie easily turned their attention to what they planned to order for lunch.

Jeremy, however, was just frowning at Ella.

"What?" she asked when her cousins had drifted into their preferred line — Jamie went for ice cream, Beth for her burger. "What's going on?" he asked quietly. "What do you care what that girl is doing?"

"It's *who* she's *doing*," Ella snapped. "We saw them together the other night, remember?"

"I know. I'm not an idiot." But he smiled at her, and shook his head. "So why do you care that your sister's roommate is another notch on Peter the Waiter's bedpost?"

Ella felt her heart catch.

"You know him?"

"Of course I know *of* him," Jeremy said. He shrugged. "Pebble Beach isn't that big."

Jeremy knew Peter.

That was so weird, to think about the possibility of Jeremy knowing things about her before he'd met her, but Ella brushed it away. There were more important things to worry about. Besides, Jeremy couldn't have known too much about her or he wouldn't still be here. She was sure of that.

"Well, Kelsi used to date him," she said. "I just think it's really trashy and gross that Taryn would do this to Kelsi."

"Does Kelsi know about it?"

"Not yet," Ella said. She made a face. "She'll be devastated."

Lowering her voice to a whisper, Ella told him about how she'd followed Taryn the night before, what she'd seen, and how there was no way to pretend it wasn't happening. Taryn really was doing this to Kelsi.

"Okay." He cocked his head as his brown eyes searched her face. "But you seem really invested, El. And a little bit insane. I mean, you actually *followed* her? And then *spied* on her?"

It did make her sound like a raving lunatic, actually, when he put it like that.

"I don't like it when people hurt my sister!" Ella exclaimed, knowing that she was coming off defensively.

"I don't know. It seems more personal," Jeremy countered, looking at her quizzically.

"No, it's just that I . . ." Ella started, but then she stopped. She couldn't bring herself to tell him that she had hooked up with Peter after he had just barely broken things off with Kelsi. "It's nothing," Ella finished. "I just don't want to see Kelsi get hurt, that's all. Especially by her boyfriend's sister."

Jeremy smiled at her for a moment, and then sweetly touched her hand as he got up to get their lunches.

Ella hated lying to Jeremy, but looking at him, she just couldn't bear to tell him the truth. And between choosing the truth and having Jeremy leave her in disgust or hiding it and dealing with her own angst, Ella chose the latter.

And it nearly broke her heart.

Beth loved the cold, wet snap of the early morning in Pebble Beach. She got up when the light was just sneaking in through the pine trees. She liked to imagine the sun hitting Cadillac Mountain up north in Acadia National Park, then slipping down the coast to heat up the gray air just as she stretched outside her cabin and began her run.

This morning, Beth headed down the dirt road, then swung away from the main village of Pebble Beach. Once she passed the mile marker, she turned toward the forest trail.

That was where she met up with Jimmy each day.

Beth grinned widely when she entered the forest, because it was always so much fun to see him there. Waiting for her, his eyes bright, equally pleased to see her.

So far, everything with Jimmy was going great, which Beth almost didn't want to let herself think about for fear of jinxing it. They'd had a bunch of very casual, friendly activities. Not dates, Beth thought, because there had been no kissing, or even a hint of kissing. Just a lot of hanging out, doing the healthy, sporty things Beth loved.

Jimmy could swim for ages in the chilly ocean without getting winded. He knew some cool hiking trails that led to secret lakes Beth had never seen before. And he still wanted to meet in the woods every morning and start the day with a few miles.

"Looking good," was all he said this morning, as he fell into place beside Beth.

"You, too," she replied, and then they just ran, letting the woods wake up all around them.

They were almost finished with their loop when Jimmy turned to look at her, his eyes glinting with mischief.

"I'll race you back into town," he said. "Loser buys coffee."

"I don't feel like racing," Beth lied casually, and then took off with a burst of speed, laughing when she heard Jimmy's shouted protest behind her.

"That was unfair!" he yelled.

"You only think so because you can't catch me," Beth threw over her shoulder.

But those were words she was forced to eat two miles

and a defeat later. When she finally caught up with him outside the Wharf Café, Jimmy was looking especially smug. He handed her an iced latte.

"I thought *I* had to buy the coffee," she said. Or tried to say, as she was still out of breath.

"Nah." Jimmy tilted his head to one side. "I think it's cute that you thought you could beat me."

He smiled before she could protest, and Beth's annoyance died a quick death. He had such a great smile.

"Well, thanks," she replied with an eye roll, reaching for the latte.

"And in general," Jimmy added softly, "I just think you're cute."

Beth smiled back at him, sipping her latte and feeling her heart give a kick.

And with a perfect summer day all around them and the smell of the sea on her skin, Beth almost forgot that she'd lost the race.

"Where's Jimmy Neutron?" George asked later that day, while the two of them sat on the edge of the pier. They had stolen Beth's uncle's fishing poles and were casting lines off the end of the wooden walkway. George called it "Making like Huck Finn," which Beth thought was funny, even though she now sort of wanted to push him into the water.

"Excuse me?" she questioned, raising her eyebrows.

"Your new pal," George replied. "Isn't he surgically attached to you throughout the day?"

"Unlike some people," Beth said pointedly, "Jimmy actually works. He's a camp counselor at that baseball camp out on the coast road." She flicked some hair out of her eyes. "And your new girlfriend? What does she do again?"

"Well, she tans," George replied. "She applies enough sunscreen to block out the sun entirely, and then she lies on the beach. I don't actually see the point."

Beth kept her gaze on her fishing line, and the dappled water below. She'd hung out with Larissa a few more times, and thought she was okay — in a hyper, giggly sort of way. Beth didn't see any particular spark between George and Larissa — she just saw that Larissa thought George was funny. And George *was* funny, so she guessed that worked out.

"It makes perfect sense to me," Beth told George with a shrug, even though she secretly agreed with him.

George rolled his eyes and wiggled his fishing pole between his palms.

"Girls are weird," he said.

"Hey, guys," came a voice from behind them.

Beth turned to smile up at Jimmy, who was freshly showered after his long day of summer camp, and looking extra cute in his long-sleeved T-shirt, cargo shorts, and flip-flops.

Jimmy smiled at George.

George smiled back, but it didn't make it to his eyes.

"Catch anything?" Jimmy asked George, sitting down between the two of them.

"Not yet," George said. "But I'm working on my lies. You know, to tell my family. You can't fish if you don't lie."

Beth laughed. Jimmy looked at George for a moment, then turned his head and looked at Beth.

"What are you doing tonight?" he asked.

"I'm up for anything," Beth replied happily. "George said there's this outdoor concert out by —"

"Because I have two tickets to the Portland Sea Dogs game," Jimmy said, his excitement coloring his voice. "Want to go with me?"

Later, it occurred to Beth that George might not have completely enjoyed watching some other guy ask out his ex-girlfriend. Not because he still had feelings for Beth, of course, since he was with Larissa, but because . . . well, it was weird. But by the time Beth thought of that, she was sitting in Hadlock Field in Portland, staring at a replica of Fenway's Green Monster from across the baseball diamond.

And the truth was, she was having a great time.

There were warm hot dogs covered in yellow mustard and occasional sips from Jimmy's cold beer. Jimmy knew the complete stats of every single player on the field, and managed to share all that information without sounding like

SportsCenter. It was a beautiful summer evening, the home team was kicking butt, and she was out with a boy who looked at her like she was the only girl in existence. When he wasn't shouting along with the crowd, that is.

It seemed like every time their eyes met, they held on to each other for a few extra moments. Like it was hard to look away. Beth had to remind herself to keep breathing, and she couldn't get the smile off her face.

The Sea Dogs were ahead at the seventh inning stretch. Beth jumped to her feet and threw her arms over her head.

"Come on!" she cried, tugging at Jimmy's arm. "You have to sing!"

"I have a terrible voice," he protested.

"That's the whole point!" Beth tipped her head back and shouted out the words to "Take Me Out to the Ball Game," which she thought must have been imprinted on her brain when she was very little, because she might not have been to a baseball game in a long time, but she could remember every single word. Not only that, she *loved* singing it.

Jimmy stood next to her, adding his voice to the crowd's, and Beth loved the feel of his strong arm around her shoulders. It made everything seem magical.

As the last notes of the organ died away, Beth leaned over to watch a commotion near the dugout. The Portland players had released a pig onto the baseball diamond. Which would have been strange and silly enough, but this particular pig had a rake attached to its back, so it could rake the dirt of the infield.

Beth laughed so hard she felt tears well up in the corners of her eyes, and had to sag against Jimmy for support.

"How could you not tell me this was coming?" she asked when she could finally speak again. "What *is* this? Is it, like, a Portland tradition?"

But when she wiped at her eyes to clear them, she saw that Jimmy wasn't laughing. He looked serious and had a weird look in his eyes.

"What's wrong?" she asked, sobering.

"Nothing," he replied, and smirked. "I just don't think it's very funny, that's all. But you look pretty when you laugh that hard." He smiled and turned back to the game, but Beth winced. She didn't know how someone couldn't find the humor in something so inherently ridiculous. She smiled briefly, thinking that George would have thought the pig was hilarious. Then Beth looked over at Jimmy, sighed, and finished watching the game.

"I'm so glad we won!" Beth rejoiced, walking out of the stadium and into the heat of the packed parking lot to Jimmy's car. She had a good time at the game and had mostly forgotten the earlier incident about the pig.

Beth looked over at Jimmy who was, once again, strangely silent. "Wasn't it a great game?"

Jimmy grinned. "I can't believe that you want to talk about the game. Right now, I don't care about baseball at all."

"What do you —" Beth started, confused. But then he slid his palm around to the nape of her neck, pulled her close, and kissed her, hard.

Beth gasped. And then she kissed him back. Electric heat shot over and through her like she'd been hit by lightning, and she moved closer, angling her head for a better fit.

As people swarmed around them on the way back to their cars, Beth and Jimmy stumbled and he gently pinned her against the car for support. Jimmy kissed her lips again, gently this time. Then he followed the line of her chin down to her neck, which he kissed very softly, taking Beth's breath away. When he pulled back, he was smiling.

"We should go . . . somewhere else," Beth said. She shivered from the kisses and the sudden lack of body heat.

Jimmy grinned and kissed her again, knowingly. "Sure. Only if you promise not to talk about baseball."

Kelsi was pretty sure that she knew every single inch of I-95 that stretched between New York City and Maine, and could, if asked, draw the route in extensive detail from memory.

Which, she realized as she sat in Bennett's apartment, did not make the prospect of making the trip again appealing in any way.

When Bennett came out of the kitchen, Kelsi was sitting on his bed in the direct path of the air conditioner in the window, staring glumly at her backpack.

"I know," he said at once, coming over and climbing onto the bed next to her. "I don't want you to go, either."

Kelsi smiled at him, but she wasn't sure she managed to hide the weariness she felt. She didn't want to make the long drive back to Maine. She didn't want to wake up tomorrow morning and start missing him all over again. It seemed like everything was way harder than it should have been this summer.

But she knew that getting upset about it would only make their good-byes worse than they had to be. Kelsi took a deep breath and forced herself to smile.

"It's okay," she said. She reached over to touch his cheek, and then lay her head on his shoulder. "I'll see you next weekend."

But before he said anything, she knew, because he went silent and still.

Slowly, she sat back up, and searched his face.

"What is it?" she asked. She didn't get hysterical. She didn't even really change her expression. If anything, she just felt kind of numb.

"I don't think I'll be able to come up to Maine this weekend," Bennett said. He looked at her, then down at the floor. "Carlos is freaking out over this exhibit we're putting together. He thinks everything we have so far looks totally collegiate. I don't see me getting away for at least a few weeks."

"A few *weeks*," Kelsi repeated. As if repeating the words would help her make sense of them.

"The exhibit is coming up fast, and Carlos is determined to get that prima donna from Artspace to write him a good review," Bennett explained, his brow slightly furrowed.

Kelsi didn't necessarily know exactly what he was talking about, but she recognized that scornful tone of voice. It seemed like she was hearing it more and more these days. When had Bennett become so judgmental?

"Okay," Kelsi said, feeling as if she might just break down and sob. "You have to concentrate on work stuff. I guess I'll just see you when I see you."

"Don't worry," Bennett said then, kissing her. "It's all going to be okay."

And for a while, sitting on his bed and kissing him, wrapping herself around him, it was.

But then, inevitably, Kelsi found herself behind the wheel of her car, inching up I-95.

Don't worry, he'd said. The fact was, Kelsi worried over everything these days. What Bennett was thinking when he made his snide art observations, for example. Somehow it made Kelsi wonder if he'd started seeing her differently, too. At some point, he was bound to think she was *collegiate,* too, wasn't he?

Or maybe he just wished she were around more.

Kelsi felt completely torn. On the one hand, she loved her lazy summers in Maine with her cousins and wouldn't want to trade them. But on the other hand, there was no particular *reason* for her to be there. She could just as easily be spending her summer in Manhattan with Bennett — and for all intents and purposes, she was. She just seemed to go back up to Pebble Beach to do her laundry.

A twelve-hour drive to do laundry and look at the bay? Ridiculous. Not to mention, it was getting harder and harder to leave Bennett. It actually hurt physically. Especially when she had no idea when she'd get to see him again.

Kelsi plugged in her iPod, cranked up Joan Baez for some old-school angst, and tried to concentrate on the drive.

Many hours later, Kelsi tried to shake off her blue mood as she turned onto the coast road that led into Pebble Beach. She still felt exhilarated when she rolled down her windows and let the salt air rush into the car. The Maine night was inky. As she turned the car away from the water and headed toward the Tuttle cottages, she could hear the lonely spooky sounds of the loons calling to one another from the inland lake, and it made her sigh.

It was so beautiful, and yet she wished she were back in New York City.

She pulled her car in behind the cottage, got out, and stretched.

When Kelsi went inside, the cottage was hushed and empty. It was late, so Kelsi supposed her dad was sleeping. There was no sign of Ella, which wasn't surprising. Taryn had told Kelsi that when Kelsi was away, Ella practically lived at her boyfriend's house. It still surprised Kelsi that Ella had managed to hold on to one boyfriend for so long, but she was happy for her sister. She liked Jeremy.

Kelsi walked back into the bedroom, and was surprised to find Taryn there, just sitting on the bed.

"Are you meditating?" Kelsi asked, laughing. "I don't think I've ever seen you sit so still."

Taryn looked up at Kelsi with a strange expression on her face, but almost immediately she wiped it clean and went blank instead.

"I'm running out," she said quickly, tucking her cell phone into the pocket of her cargo pants. "I'm already late." She jumped to her feet.

Confused, Kelsi put out a hand as Taryn charged past her. Taryn stopped, and looked at Kelsi with that same blank expression.

"Are you okay?" Kelsi asked. "Did something happen?"

"I'm late," Taryn repeated, and there was no mistaking the coldness in her voice.

Bewildered and still wound up from the drive, words failed Kelsi.

So she just moved aside and let Taryn go.

Kelsi slept for almost fourteen hours, and when she woke up, she felt like a different person.

Puttering around in the kitchen, she decided to make breakfast while she mulled over Taryn's weirdness the night before.

Probably nothing, she concluded. Everyone got a little weird sometimes, and Kelsi had discovered that when Taryn got stressed, she often got a little crazy.

That was what she told herself right up until her best friend walked into the kitchen, visibly flinched when she saw Kelsi standing there, turned on her heel, and walked right out.

"Taryn!" Kelsi called out in disbelief, leaving her tofu scramble to burn on the stove.

She ran over to the door and saw that the other girl had stopped walking, though she didn't turn around.

"What's going on?" Kelsi asked Taryn's back. "Did I do something to piss you off?" But that was ridiculous — they hadn't even been in the same state for days.

"I forgot that I have to meet someone," Taryn said, still without turning. "I have to go."

And, again, she did.

Kelsi barely registered the fact that Ella had appeared from the sunporch, looking rumpled and sleepy-eyed. She watched Taryn walk away, and then she looked at Kelsi.

"What's up with her?" Ella asked with a frown, slipping into the kitchen.

"I have no idea," Kelsi murmured.

The late afternoon sun poured golden across the traffic on Route 1, making it seem beautiful instead of annoying — which traffic usually was. Ella leaned back in the passenger seat of Jeremy's car, and curled her long, bare legs up beneath her.

"This was a good idea," she told Jeremy, reaching over to put her hand on his knee as he drove.

"I can't believe it's August and we haven't had lobster rolls yet," Jeremy said. "*What* have we been thinking?"

Ella knew what she'd been thinking: that things were strange and upsetting with Kelsi, and that Kelsi's best friend was betraying her. Possibly she was doing so *at this very moment*. And that she had lied to Jeremy and was keeping a huge secret from him.

But Jeremy had probably been thinking about his job.

And Ella. That was one of the reasons she loved him so much, the fact that he was always thinking of her. Ella was used to guys obsessing over her, but Jeremy wasn't like that. He worried for her.

He'd gotten off work at noon today, and had told her to go home and shower off the salt and sand of the beach, because they were going on a date that required a road trip.

Ella had complied happily. She'd found her favorite pair of Bermudas — cut to emphasize the curve of her hips — and paired them with wickedly high espadrilles and a deep purple tank top. She looked like L. L. Bean gone naughty.

Which Jeremy had fully appreciated, of course.

"I don't know what you're wearing," he said the moment the screen door slapped shut behind them on their way out of Ella's house, "but it's already driving me crazy."

He'd grabbed her hips with his hands and pulled her to him, covering her mouth with his.

Ella poured herself into the kiss, wiggling closer to him and arching her back so she could feel him press tighter into her.

God, she loved touching him.

They'd barely made it into his car — only breaking apart from a blistering hot kiss when Beth and Jimmy interrupted them by walking around the side of Beth's cottage, dressed in whites and holding tennis rackets.

143

"You might want to get a room," Beth had suggested, swinging her racket for emphasis. "Maybe one a little farther away from your entire extended family."

Jimmy had just watched them, swinging his racket as if he was hitting a tennis ball. If he was offended by the PDA he'd just witnessed, he didn't mention it.

Ella and Jeremy looked at each other and laughed, and then kissed once more. But then they'd jumped in the car. The next person to come around the side of the building might very well be Ella's dad, and no one wanted *that*.

The moment Jeremy had started heading south out of town on Route 1, Ella had known where they were going. And she was thrilled. Lobster rolls at Red's were becoming a Jeremy and Ella tradition.

"What made you think of this today?" she asked him now, as they entered the town of Wiscasset.

"You've seemed sad lately," Jeremy said, smiling at her. "And you know I hate that. It's, like, my duty to make you smile, and I like that." Ella knew that she had been a little distracted recently, feeling guilty about not telling him the truth about Peter. Part of her knew that it was the right decision, but keeping something from Jeremy was tearing her apart.

Ella looked over at him, and then reached across the space between them to trace his lips with her fingers.

"And you're good at making me smile," she told him.

"I love you," Jeremy said simply, his smile crooked and perfect.

Ella let out a sigh of contentment, and looked around at the pretty town, where traffic was always at a crawl, and tourists browsed through antique shops while walking up and down Main Street's brick sidewalk. Here it was easy to forget about the whole Kelsi-Taryn-Peter drama, but every time she looked over at Jeremy, so perfect and so in love with her, she felt those little pangs of guilt again.

Jeremy parked, and then they walked hand in hand toward the little roadside shack that was Red's — easily identifiable from far away, thanks to the long line in front of it.

As a rule, Ella was opposed to waiting in line. But this afternoon was different. Jeremy was there with her, tickling her when she got impatient and making her giggle before she swatted at him.

"I will beat you down," she warned him at one point through more giggles. "Stop tickling me!"

"It's that snort that kills me," Jeremy said, completely ignoring Ella and tickling her again.

And then it was finally their turn at the window, which was just as well, because Ella could tell that the old couple behind them were growing a little impatient with their wrestling.

Luckily, Ella didn't care what they thought.

Jeremy ordered two lobster rolls, and Ella watched through the window as the woman picked out the best meat and threw rolls onto the grill. Red's lobster rolls weren't salad-y (which Ella found revolting), they were just overstuffed with lobster meat. Butter and mayo came on the side.

When their rolls were ready, Jeremy held the plates and they snagged prime seats on the deck, sandwiched between the Sheepscot River and the traffic on Route 1.

They sat side by side and looked out over the water. Jeremy fed Ella succulent bites of sweet lobster drenched in butter, and kissed her fingers when she did the same for him.

"This is perfect," Ella whispered. "Just what I needed. Thank you."

"You know I would do anything for you," Jeremy said, his dark eyes crinkling a little bit at the corners.

Ella looked at him and saw all of that love in his eyes. She felt something swell in her, something so intense she almost wanted to cry. Ella knew in that moment that she had to tell Jeremy everything. She loved him too much to have something this big between them. "Jeremy . . ." she began, not really knowing how to begin.

Jeremy looked at her expectantly. Suddenly she blurted it out, unable to stop the mess spewing from her lips. "I kind of had a thing with Peter, too. Right after he and Kelsi broke up. Like, within hours. She stopped talking to me when she found out last summer."

Jeremy blinked, and shook his head. Some emotion passed across his face, and he shook his head again, silently looking out over the harbor.

"Please say something," Ella begged, after a moment of terrible silence. Part of her wanted him to say something horrible, so she could yell or scream or *something*.

"I don't know . . ." he said, looking disgusted. "I mean, what do you want me to say?"

"I don't know!" Ella retorted, suddenly feeling exhausted by the stress of the whole thing. "I wanted you to know because I love you. But I can't apologize to you for my past. And I shouldn't have to." Even if the past repulsed her, too.

"Hey," he said, angrily. "Don't get mad at me. I'm not the one who hooked up with Peter the Tool."

Ella knew that she had messed up. She had selfishly blurted it out and now she was going to lose him. She had to look away as small tears began to fall down her cheeks.

"Ella, I'm sorry. Please look at me."

"I don't want to," she whispered.

"Look, Ella. I love you," Jeremy said, and he took her hand again, so she looked at him. His eyes were serious and he started speaking, slowly. "It kills me to think of you with another guy. And I especially hate thinking about you with Peter."

Ella gulped, trying to force down the sobs that were in her throat.

Jeremy continued. "But I know that it was all in the past. Honestly, I don't care what happened before me, okay? I really don't."

"Really?" Ella asked, quietly. "Because nothing before you matters."

"I know. It's hard for me to hear, but I know."

Ella sighed in relief and leaned in against him. Jeremy moved closer to her and put his arm around her shoulders. They looked over the water as the sun began to go down. "But, El," he said. "I think this thing about Taryn and Peter has to stop," he said gently. "It's like you're jealous or something."

"I am *not* jealous," Ella replied immediately.

"Not about Peter. About Taryn and Kelsi," Jeremy said in the same easy tone. "I know you feel like she's taking your sister away from you. Maybe you want to make up for what you did, but Taryn isn't you. This isn't your business."

He didn't understand, Ella thought, looking away. He couldn't possibly, but she also didn't know how to explain it to him, either. She didn't say anything, but luckily, neither did he. They just sat in silence, Ella in Jeremy's arms. They looked out over the water and the old, decaying fishing boats, breathing in the cool sea air, and Ella felt lucky and confused all at once.

16

It had been raining for almost a week, and Beth decided everyone had gone completely stir-crazy.

She stood at the screen door of her cottage, staring out at the grassy picnic area, which was now reduced to mud and rivulets. Sheets of rain obscured the view and made it all a little bit blurry.

Okay, *she* had gone stir-crazy, anyway.

The first day it poured had been fun. The little cousins jumped in the puddles, and the adults played card games while Beth, Kelsi, Jamie, and Ella had lounged around reading, watching movies, or catching up on sleep.

By the third day of unrelenting rain, however, Beth had suffered a severe sense of humor failure. She missed her morning runs with Jimmy. Because he worked rain or shine, Beth still had to sit around all day waiting for him.

Not, of course, that there weren't a million things to do around the Tuttle compound, Beth thought ruefully. Jamie had been knitting what seemed like entire sweaters, but then had randomly ditched Beth yesterday when they were supposed to go to Bed, Bath & Beyond for a dorm shopping spree.

Like it wasn't weird enough to be off buying things like hot plates and coffeemakers, all in preparation for some big new life Beth couldn't entirely picture in her head. She had been excited to pick out shower supplies, but at the same time, nervous. Change was hard. Especially when it involved things Beth had always taken for granted, like having her own bathroom and her mom doing her laundry.

Kelsi and Taryn, meanwhile, had been holed up in their bedroom with the entire seventh season DVD set of *Buffy the Vampire Slayer*. When Beth had peeked in yesterday — looking for Jamie — they'd both been weeping.

And Ella, alarmingly, claimed that she was *reading* in bed, and had barricaded herself on the sunporch.

Which meant that Beth had nothing to do but sit around all day, and Beth wasn't the kind of person who *liked* to sit around for days on end. She liked to *do* things. Normally, she loved her family's summer cottage, but today she felt trapped in it. Forced inactivity made her feel like screaming.

Which was very nearly what she did when George slammed in through the front door, like Kramer from *Seinfeld*, which Beth assumed George still watched in nightly reruns.

"The thing is," she said, hearing the crankiness in her own voice and not really caring since it was just George, "I'm not Jerry Seinfeld and you actually don't live next door."

"Really? This shocks me," George said.

"My point is, you could call ahead. Or, you know, knock?"

"Because you're so busy," George mocked her.

He stripped off the neon-yellow rain slicker he was wearing and they both watched as water cascaded from it across the floor. Underneath, he was wearing a long-sleeved T-shirt and cargo pants. And extremely muddy boots, which he left next to the puddle he'd just made.

Beth sighed as if she found him unbearably annoying, which made George laugh. In truth, she was happy to see him. He'd been sort of MIA lately.

"What have you been up to?" Beth asked, getting to her feet. "Please tell me it's been something fun, because I've hit complete cabin fever here," she continued gloomily, aiming her words over her shoulder as she headed into the kitchen to grab the roll of paper towels. Heading back out to the living room, she tossed the roll at George.

Predictably, he bobbled the roll of towels in the air and ended up batting it to the ground.

He was such an idiot. Beth felt a mix of affection and exasperation snake through her.

"Your problem is that you view the rain as your enemy," George announced. He tore off a paper towel square and ran it over his damp head, instead of at the huge puddle at his feet.

"The rain is fine," Beth contradicted him, just because she felt like being difficult. "You, however, I'm not so sure about."

"You manage to find things to do all winter long," George pointed out. "You don't have to sit here, being gloomy."

"If you're not going to be entertaining, you can leave," Beth told him, flopping back down on the couch.

George rolled his eyes and flopped into the armchair.

They sat there for a long moment in silence, listening to the rain batter the roof of Beth's cottage. Beth turned her gaze up toward the ceiling, knowing without having to go look that there would be a pool forming in the cellar and an inevitable leak in her parents' bathroom. Everything was damp, as if the cottage was a sponge and just soaked in the weather.

"You still seeing Jimmy Neutron, Boy Genius?" George asked after a minute.

Beth eyed him.

"We've been on a few dates, yeah," she said, pretending to be indifferent. The dates had actually all been great, and kissing Jimmy was amazing, but she didn't think George really wanted that information.

"That's cool," George said, his knee jerking in a staccato rhythm. Beth realized she still thought it was kind of cute that he was such a fidgeter. So she figured his new girlfriend probably thought so, too.

"How are things with Larissa?" she asked. "She seems really nice. You guys will have so much fun in Pittsburgh."

George shrugged.

"I don't know," he said.

"What do you mean?" Beth had to wonder if she sounded too interested when George looked at her. But she didn't know how else to sound. She didn't know what the rules were when it came to talking to her ex about his new relationship.

"She's definitely a nice girl," George said slowly. "Don't get me wrong. But I don't know if I really . . ." He shrugged again. "I just don't think she's right for me, you know?"

"Why not?" Beth asked.

"I'm not sure I can offer, like, a full analysis here, Beth," George said. "You either feel it or you don't, right?" Then he grinned. "The G-Man has high standards."

Beth rolled her eyes, but couldn't hold back her laughter.

"Spare me," she said.

"You know it's true," he retorted.

"I know you're a dork," she threw right back at him, and then tossed a pillow at him, too, as punctuation.

*　　*　　*

"Does George come around a lot?" Jimmy asked the next night when the rain had stopped. It was still gray, cold, and overcast, but at least it wasn't raining. When Jimmy had shown up after camp let out, Beth had practically tackled him with joy. His cheeks were a little bit flushed, his eyes sparkled green against the gray evening, and Beth wanted to rub his close-cut auburn hair against her palms.

Now they were walking along the coast road, where the water crashed against the beach and the wind kicked through the houses and cut to the bone. No one else was out, so it was like they were the only two people alive in the world.

Jimmy had not been too excited to find George hanging out in the cottage with Beth again.

"I think he's just bored," Beth said now, leaning forward into the wind. "He used to spend his summers with my family, so there used to be a lot more going on."

"Your family," Jimmy repeated.

"Yeah, he was like the unofficial boy cousin," Beth said. "Because we don't have one of those. Not our age, anyway."

"Give me a break, Beth," Jimmy said with a sigh.

"What?"

"You think your family is the big attraction?" He shook his head. "The guy isn't hanging out with your family. He's there to see you. What happened to that other girl he was hanging out with?"

As far as Beth knew, Jimmy had never actually met Larissa. He'd just heard Beth mention her.

"George just said she wasn't girlfriend material," Beth said with a shrug. "Whatever that means."

"I know what that means when a guy says it to another guy," Jimmy said, shooting Beth a look. "I also know what it means when a guy says it to the ex-girlfriend he can't seem to stop hanging out with."

Beth let her breath out, and tucked her hands into her jeans.

"Jimmy, we're just —"

"— friends, I know," Jimmy finished. He shook his head. "But does he know that? Seriously? Because it seems to me that he's just waiting."

"Waiting for what?" Beth asked.

"For you," Jimmy said impatiently. "Don't be *naive*, Beth."

Beth didn't know how to answer. She looked down at her muddy boots, and wished she could think of what to say.

Was George waiting? She certainly wasn't. But if she was honest, she knew that part of her had kind of liked the idea that Larissa hadn't been up to George's high standards. Because that meant that only Beth was. Surely, though, that was just normal, residual ex stuff that didn't mean anything.

She thought of how easy it was to talk to and banter with

George, to slip back into their old patterns. But she didn't still have romantic feelings for him.

Jimmy was so different from the other guys she'd known. Those guys being George, and last summer, Adam, who was a lot like George when all was said and done. Jimmy was something else entirely.

"Listen," Jimmy said. He stood there until Beth looked up, and she relaxed a little bit because he didn't seem mad or upset.

"I'm listening," she said.

"I like you," he told her, his eyes clear and, she could tell, completely sincere. "I think you like me, too, and we have a good time together."

"I think so, too," Beth said. There was something kind of amazing about having such a direct conversation. She felt electricity shoot through her.

"But I can't handle George," Jimmy said. "I tried to just roll with it, but he's always around. And he's all over you."

"He's not all over me!" Beth protested, feeling her cheeks heat up.

"He makes up excuses to touch you," Jimmy said very patiently, and Beth knew he was right.

"Okay," she conceded. "But I don't think he means anything by it. I think it's just habit."

"Tell me how I'm supposed to deal with this." Jimmy's

eyes searched hers. "Summer's almost over. Do I fight him for you? That seems pretty lame."

"There's nothing to fight about!" Beth exclaimed. She frowned, and tucked a stray golden hair behind her ear before the wind snatched it across her face.

"I'm friends with my exes, too," Jimmy said patiently. "But they don't hang out at my house, or . . ."

"George is just . . ." But Beth didn't know how to describe him anymore. She wasn't even sure why she was defending him.

"I kind of like him, to tell you the truth," Jimmy said. But he shrugged then, and let his hands fall at his sides. "But I don't want to compete with him."

Beth's head was reeling. "You're not competing with him." She took Jimmy's hands and squeezed them until he looked at her, straight in the eye. "You're not," she said again. "I don't know what's going on with George, but I do know that he and I are over. We broke up almost a year ago, and I've never regretted it."

"You're saying you're totally over this guy," Jimmy said very carefully, as if he expected her to deny it.

But Beth met his eyes. Because she knew this was right.

"Believe me," she said in the same tone, "I am completely over George."

Because she had to be.

On another gorgeous Pebble Beach day, Kelsi decided not to mope around the house, and took her frustrations out to the yard and focused them on the tetherball set. It was surprisingly therapeutic to hit the ball, sending it spinning and spinning on the end of its rope.

Kelsi was seriously considering installing a tetherball set in her dorm room next year. She had a feeling it would come in handy during finals.

She gave the ball a *whack* because she missed Bennett.

Then another, more vicious *whack* for his new Art Snob persona, which Kelsi now fully admitted to herself that she hated.

Whack for Taryn, and whatever *her* problem was these days.

Whack because Kelsi didn't know what to do with a best friend who was cold, distant, and seemed to be avoiding her.

Whack and then another, harder *whack* because when Kelsi asked, Taryn totally lied and said she didn't know what Kelsi was talking about, and that everything was fine.

Kelsi hit the ball back and forth, harder and harder, with escalating force, and then, finally, put everything she had into one last *whack*.

It was pretty satisfying to watch the cord wrap itself around the pole. She *almost* felt better about the fact that it was yet another Saturday and she wasn't with her boyfriend.

Almost.

Kelsi turned back toward the cottages.

"I wouldn't want to be that tetherball," a deep, familiar voice said. Kelsi turned and saw Bennett sitting on the nearest picnic table.

Kelsi felt herself gape at him.

She couldn't believe it.

There he was, stretched out across the bench, looking rumpled and adorable in his jeans and a Ramones T-shirt. He had stubble on his jaw, and his eyes were bloodshot behind his black glasses, but he was sitting there in all the glory of the Maine sunshine.

"I can't believe you're here!" she cried, and ran, hurling herself into his arms. She held him so close, she could actually feel his skin, and convinced herself that she wasn't dreaming. She shut her eyes and leaned into him.

"I knew I was coming up since yesterday," he whispered into her ear, pulling her down onto the bench and nuzzling her neck, "but I wanted to surprise you."

"This is the best thing that's happened all summer," she whispered back, letting him rock them both.

"Plus, I've bailed so many times, I thought you might not believe me, anyway," he admitted.

Kelsi pulled back so she could look him in the eye, and smiled. Then she kissed him.

"I'll always believe you," she promised.

Then she fell back into his arms, and felt like she could stay there forever.

It was the most perfect Saturday of the summer. Kelsi showed Bennett *everything*. She introduced him to all her relatives, and took him on a tour of Pebble Beach, from her favorite schooner spot on the rocky bluff to the pier. She pointed out the sand pits where the town held their Fourth of July clambakes, and the farmer's market where all the fresh produce was sold. They had coffee and shared a vegan cupcake at a little café Kelsi had always loved, and then walked up and down Main Street as night began to creep in.

"It's beautiful here," Bennett said. "New York feels like another lifetime."

Which Kelsi liked hearing. Because maybe realizing that there were things beyond Carlos's art world would be good for Bennett. Maybe it would remind him that he didn't have to be as pretentious and work-obsessed as it seemed everyone else in Manhattan was.

But Kelsi didn't say any of that. She didn't want to ruin the moment. So instead she just took his hand.

Later, they stood together on the edge of the pier, looking out over the water at the small, rocky islands that cluttered the bay. They were all pines and boulders, and they created fascinating shadows across the calm water, which Kelsi and Bennett took turns pointing out to each other. They stood there until the sun was completely gone, the last streaks of red and pink faded into the inky blue of the oncoming night.

Bennett sighed a little bit, and pulled Kelsi into the crook of his arm.

"This has been an amazing day. It's going to be tough to go back to New York tomorrow."

Kelsi let out a sigh of protest. "I don't want to talk about it yet," she told him. "We'll have to deal with it tomorrow."

Bennett kissed her, hard and long, and then kissed her again on her forehead.

"I love you," he said. "This summer has been so tough, but everything's going to be fine in a few weeks."

Kelsi smiled into his eyes. "I know. I'm glad," she said.

They held hands and walked back into town. They were standing on Main Street, debating whether to have dinner out or at home, when Kelsi saw a familiar figure detach from the jostling crowd outside Ahoy.

It was Taryn, who Kelsi had been expecting to run into all day. Somehow, they never had.

"She's going to freak when she sees me," Bennett predicted, laughter in his voice.

Kelsi hadn't told Bennett about the cold shoulder Taryn had been giving her. She thought that would only put him in an awkward position, and she didn't see the point in that. So she put on as big a smile as she could, fully prepared to pretend that everything was fine between her and Taryn.

"Hey there," Bennett said when Taryn drew close, her head down.

She obviously recognized his voice because she jumped, and her mouth fell open when she looked up and saw him standing there.

"Surprise," Bennett said softly.

His tone was strange, Kelsi thought — almost careful. But then she quickly forgot about that, because Taryn stiffened and looked from Bennett to Kelsi, and then back again.

"You've got to be kidding me," she said fiercely. "What are you doing here?"

"Surprising me," Kelsi said, feeling her stomach tense.

"Ease up, Taryn," Bennett suggested quietly, sounding tense.

"Whatever," Taryn snapped. She wrapped her arms around her middle. "I can't deal with this."

"Taryn —" Kelsi started, but Taryn threw up a hand and Kelsi's words died in her throat.

"Have fun," Taryn said bitterly, and then she turned on her heel and took off in the opposite direction.

For a moment, Kelsi and Bennett just stood there in the dark.

"What was *that*?" Kelsi asked, bewildered. She shook her head. "She's been acting like a weirdo for a while, you know. It's like she's mad at me about something."

"I wouldn't worry about it," Bennett said. He settled his arm around Kelsi's shoulders and kissed her ear. "In a few weeks, we'll be back in Massachusetts and everything will be back to normal."

"I don't know," Kelsi said, but Bennett kissed her again, this time on her mouth.

"Trust me," he urged her. "It's been a hard summer, but everything's going to be okay."

Kelsi wanted to believe him more than anything, so she kissed him back, and then gazed at him. He was more beautiful to her than the stars that crowded the sky above them.

"Come on," she whispered, and gave him a sexy smile. "Let's not waste our one night together in Pebble Beach."

The next morning was hard, as Bennett had to leave very early, and Kelsi got up to see him drive south, down the dirt road toward town. It was so early that she waved a hello to Beth, who emerged from her cottage already in her running gear, and looked surprised to see anyone else up and about.

Kelsi watched her cousin take off at a good speed, and then went back inside to crawl into her bed.

Much later that afternoon, she was awake again — but just barely. She was sitting sideways out in the hammock in the backyard, talking to Bennett on the phone and contemplating the sunshine that made it through the pines to warm the grass beneath her feet.

"I'm sitting in traffic outside Danbury," he told her. "But it was worth it. Are you okay? You sound strange."

"I'm just mellow," Kelsi assured him. "Yesterday was wonderful. I'm so glad you came."

"Me, too," he agreed. Then he laughed a little bit. "Don't get so relaxed you forget to miss me," Bennett teased her. "That's unacceptable."

Kelsi laughed, and enjoyed some highly satisfying mushy talk with him. So it was particularly embarrassing when she hung up to find Taryn standing there.

"How's Bennett?" Taryn asked, giving Kelsi an icy stare.

"He's fine," Kelsi replied uneasily. "Just stuck in traffic. Why?"

"He didn't tell you, did he?" Taryn blurted out. Her cheeks were very pink.

"I don't know what you're talking about!" Kelsi felt helpless. "What's going on with you?! What was last night all about?"

"I get that this isn't my business, but I can't believe you would want him to throw his life away," Taryn said in the same hard tone — which, Kelsi realized belatedly, was masking the fact that Taryn was very upset.

"You have to tell me what's going on, Taryn," Kelsi finally said firmly. "Or I can't contribute to this conversation."

Taryn took a deep breath, and then met Kelsi's eyes.

"Carlos offered Bennett a residency in his gallery, for next year. It's an unheard-of honor."

"That's *amazing*!" Kelsi agreed. She frowned at the phone in her hand. "I don't understand why he hasn't told me —"

"Because he turned it down," Taryn snapped. She took a ragged breath. "He turned it down, Kelsi, even though Carlos hasn't offered anyone a residency in years! He turned it down because he wants to stay in Massachusetts. With you."

Kelsi just stared at Taryn, uncomprehending.

"But that's . . ." She couldn't finish.

"Career suicide," Taryn finished for her. Her mouth tightened. "He won't listen to me. So it's up to you. What do you think he should choose? His entire future? Or you?"

Ella watched Taryn storm away from the hammock, headed in the direction of the beach.

She realized she was holding her breath, waiting to see Kelsi's reaction to the news.

Because she'd engineered the confrontation and because she was just hoping Kelsi would take it better than she had last summer when the person who'd betrayed her was Ella.

Ella had been watching the cold war between Taryn and Kelsi develop ever since she'd stumbled into it the morning Kelsi returned from New York. The last few weeks had been excruciating — Taryn had been avoiding Kelsi, who, in turn, just looked confused. And worse, hurt. Things had been better briefly when Bennett had shown up yesterday, but Ella suspected that Kelsi's good mood probably left with him in his rented Impala.

Ella hadn't been able to bear it another second, so when Taryn wafted into the living room earlier that afternoon, Ella had taken matters into her own hands.

"You need to tell her," she had announced.

Taryn had looked startled. As well she might. As far as Ella knew, Taryn had no idea that Ella was onto her.

"Um, okay," she'd said, acting as if she hadn't known what Ella was talking about.

"Kelsi deserves to know what's going on," Ella had told her. She couldn't remember ever having been more serious.

Taryn had stared at her for a long while. Ella had been afraid for a moment that she would demand to know how Ella had figured everything out, but she didn't. She just shook her head.

"You're a little bit spooky," she said, which Ella might have taken offense to, until Taryn continued, "but you're absolutely right."

Maybe she *was* right, Ella thought now, but that didn't make her feel any better if Kelsi's heart was shattered *all over* again.

Finally, Kelsi rose from the hammock, and turned so Ella could see her face. She looked dazed more than anything else. But not, Ella was relieved to see, in pieces.

Kelsi walked in the cottage door and didn't seem to notice that her sister was sitting right there until Ella shifted position on the couch.

"Oh," she said, distracted. "I didn't see you."

"It's better that you know," Ella said hurriedly.

Kelsi focused on her and shook her head.

"Are you kidding me?" she cried, color flooding her cheeks. "Did Bennett tell everyone on the planet except me?"

Ella frowned. "What does Bennett have to do with anything? I'm talking about Peter."

"Peter?" Kelsi's brow furrowed. It was like she didn't know who Peter was. Like she'd forgotten him. Ella rushed on.

"Your roommate is seeing him. In alleys, apparently." It was maybe a little bitchier than necessary, but Ella was off-balance. If Taryn hadn't told Kelsi about Peter, what *had* they been talking about out by the hammock?

"Oh," Kelsi said, her forehead creasing in confusion. "*That* Peter." She blinked as if to clear her head. "I can't imagine why you'd want to talk about that guy, El, but I can't do it right now. I have to lie down."

Ella was at a loss.

"Did you hear me?" she demanded. "Taryn is, like, *actively* dating him! They were all over each other in the Lighthouse!"

"I don't need details, Ella," Kelsi said impatiently. She

pushed her hair back from her forehead. "And what do you care what Peter does?"

Ella gaped at her. She actually felt her mouth drop open.

"Why don't *you* care?" she threw back at Kelsi.

"I told her he was a player," Kelsi said dismissively, and waved one hand in the air to underscore her disinterest. "Taryn can handle herself."

She knew.

Ella literally couldn't take that in. Her body shook a little bit, and her ears popped, like she'd just gotten off an airplane.

But her voice still sounded kind of normal.

"You knew?" she asked, with a little squeak at the end.

"What?" Kelsi's eyes narrowed as she searched Ella's face. "Of course I knew. Why are we talking about this, anyway?"

"Because I don't get it!" Ella cried. The fact that she was upset seemed to finally dawn on Kelsi, who frowned. But Ella just kept going. "Why don't you care? Why aren't you outraged that Taryn would do this to you?"

Now Kelsi looked like she was at a loss.

"Do *what* to me?" she sputtered, and Ella could see that her sister had no idea what was happening.

"Let me be sure I understand this," Ella said shakily. "So when you found out what happened with Peter and me a whole *year* after the fact, that was so awful that it completely ripped us apart. But when *Taryn* has a full-on *fling* with the same guy, it's all good. Because *Taryn* is so wonderful that no matter what she does, you adore her. Is that it?"

Kelsi sighed. "Okay, you're kind of jealous of her," she began in that long-suffering tone that Ella hated. The one that meant that Kelsi thought she was a complete pain in the ass.

"I am not *jealous* of her!" Ella cried, completely losing her cool. "I just don't see why when I do something, it's the end of the world, but when she does the *exact same thing,* except even *worse,* you don't give a shit!"

"It is not the same thing!" Kelsi snapped. Then she closed her eyes. "I'm not going to fight with you about this. I don't even understand why you care! It's none of your business, Ella."

"Yeah, I can see that," Ella said bitterly. Her hurt feelings from the whole summer rose up in her like nausea. "Nothing you do is my business anymore. Now that you have the great and wonderful Taryn, why should you care about anyone else? You've barely even been here this summer, Kelsi. And you spend every one of the five minutes a week you actually are here with your college roommate — you know, the one you *lived with all year* — instead of even *pretending* to hang out with your family. Why did you even bother to come to Pebble Beach at all?!"

"You are unbelievable," Kelsi replied slowly, her eyes wide. "I don't even know what to say!"

"You don't know what to say or do about anything!" Ella yelled at her. "When you're here it's like you're on a different planet! Did I miss the part where we suddenly don't even talk? You look right through me! Have you even noticed the fact that I'm sleeping on a pullout couch this summer like a loser so that you can install your stupid friend in *my* bedroom?"

Kelsi put out both her hands, as if to ward Ella off. "I can't deal with this right now!" she said, her voice rising. "You don't understand. Bennett has made this incredibly —"

"Oh, right, *Bennett*," Ella interrupted with a roll of her eyes. "Because *he's* a winner."

"What did Bennett ever do to you?" Kelsi demanded.

"I, personally, couldn't care less about Bennett," Ella informed Kelsi angrily. "But he's spent the whole summer breaking plans with you, and every time you come back from New York you're more and more miserable. What's there for me to like?"

"Maybe you didn't notice that he was *here*, like, five hours ago?"

"For the first time all summer," Ella snapped back. "And I bet you'll be miserable all over again before nightfall!"

"I'm miserable because I want to be with him, Ella," Kelsi threw at her, furious. "I'm *in love* with him! I think about him all the time, I feel like I won't make it until the next time we have sex again, I feel like I can't breathe —"

"Wait — *what* did you say?"

Because Ella could not possibly have heard that right.

"Forget it," Kelsi said angrily. "You wouldn't understand."

She clearly didn't understand what *she'd* said. Or Ella had misheard her. Nothing else made sense.

But Ella had to be sure.

"Did you say until you have sex? *Again?*"

Kelsi looked flushed. "I don't know what I said."

But Ella wasn't going to let it go.

"So, you've slept together," she said softly, feeling young and small, and hating it.

They stared at each other across the living room and, it seemed to Ella, the entire span of their childhood.

"Yes," Kelsi said finally. "I have had sex with Bennett."

Ella nodded. She ran her tongue over her teeth and then nodded again. "When?" she asked.

"The first time was a couple of months ago," Kelsi said. "But I don't —"

"A couple of months ago," Ella repeated, "and you didn't tell me. Your virginity was this *huge* thing to you for *years*, and you didn't even tell me that you lost it."

She felt like such an idiot. She remembered sitting in the kitchen earlier this summer, trying to get Kelsi to open up about boys and sex. She'd thought it was Kelsi's same old problem of being pressured. She couldn't believe how stupid she'd been or that Kelsi had let her blunder around like that. Ella felt hot tears sting her throat. She wanted to curl up in a ball and cry.

Kelsi groaned. "I know this seems like a big deal, but really, I didn't mean to not tell you. I just didn't have time."

"But there was enough time to fill Taryn in on the details of what went down with me and Peter," Ella snapped. "Summer's almost over, Kelsi. You were *never* going to tell me."

That just hung there.

And the longer it hung there, the more Ella knew that she was right.

It was awful.

"You're making this into a much bigger thing than it is, El," Kelsi finally said, taking a step closer.

What she didn't say was that Ella was wrong.

And it was like Ella finally saw everything for the first time.

Kelsi liked Taryn better. There was no competition. Taryn had already won. Ella was just the foolish little sister, the one who didn't get the in-jokes. The one who tagged along, unwanted.

The little tramp who Kelsi didn't even include in her life anymore.

And that was how Kelsi wanted it.

"You're right. I was making it into a bigger deal than it was," Ella said finally, her tone as cold and hard as ice.

"Come on, Ella," Kelsi murmured, not quite looking at her.

"Don't worry," Ella said stiffly. "I won't make that mistake again."

And then she turned around and headed outside, as fast as she could walk with the tears blurring her eyes.

Beth had spent days planning out what she was going to say, but when she saw George waiting for her at the sandwich place behind Main Street, the whole plan just sort of disappeared.

She stopped walking and looked at him for a moment. The sandwich shop took over most of the airy little court-yard that sat between the Pebble Beach Inn and the Lighthouse. Before turning into a sandwich shop this year, it had been a private home. The building was an adorable white cottage with a picket fence, and it felt like the perfect place to while away a pretty Maine afternoon.

She had asked George to meet her here, at this brand-new place that they had never been to together and which, she thought, would be completely free of any George-and-

Beth residue. He was early, which made Beth chuckle. Normally, the concept of time was completely foreign to George. He sat under the red-and-blue-striped umbrella, which was wedged in the tabletop at a lopsided angle, and was drawing shapes with his finger against the wood.

When he saw her, his narrow face broke into a wide smile.

"Bethy!" he cried. "Finally! Did you know the sandwiches at this place are, like, epic?"

"Epic?" she echoed, with an amused smirk on her face. She was unwilling to launch so quickly into what she was afraid would be a tense, horrible conversation.

"We are talking a complete and dazzling array of condiments," George was saying excitedly. "Different varieties of pickles, like, seventeen different mustards including the vile Dijonnaise that will never again pass these lips —"

"You're insane." Beth interrupted his rant by swinging her leg over the bench across from him.

"I like my mustard to be mustard and my mayo to be mayo," George retorted. "Is that so wrong?"

Beth laughed. He was so funny. He would never stop making her laugh.

But he was also her ex-boyfriend. The first guy she'd ever loved. The only one she'd slept with so far. Their relationship had gone to some dark places and sometimes that darkness still stirred in her when she looked at him. Being here in Pebble Beach should have reminded her of better times with him. Instead, she shivered, remembering their awful breakup in the freezing-cold November morning with perfect, stomach-lurching clarity.

Beth wondered if maybe they shouldn't have even tried this friend thing out in the first place. Maybe it would have been better for everyone if they'd just said good-bye and then gone their separate ways. School was starting soon, anyway. They wouldn't see each other anymore, so what did it matter if they were friends or not?

It was all so complicated.

"Earth to Bethy," George said quietly, making Beth realize she hadn't answered him. "Why are you looking at me like that?"

The fact was, Beth didn't want complicated. Her new life was set to begin in a few short weeks, and she didn't want it to be threaded through with this same regret and history. She wanted to enjoy her last summer and pretend there had never been anything before. She wanted to move on. She really, truly did.

Was that *so* wrong?

"I don't know how to say this," she began.

"Already I love this conversation," he replied. His tone was light but his brown eyes darkened.

"I just don't think this friends thing is working," she blurted, throwing it out there. "Jimmy pointed out that maybe we're kind of kidding ourselves." Or *she* was, anyway.

"Why?" George demanded. "We're terrific friends! We're exactly the way we've always been!"

"That's the problem. You and I don't know how to *just* be friends anymore," Beth said gently. "And if you think about it, we never really were."

George seemed to deflate at that, and looking away, poked at the table.

Beth was aware of how the sun beat down on the pavement beyond their table, and the laughter from a group of people to their left. But all she could see was George.

His eyes were still too dark when he looked back at her, but there was nothing angry in his face.

Beth felt her heart clutch a little bit, because she could see that he understood. He wasn't going to fight. She felt a swell of something close to disappointment in her chest, but ignored it.

"I guess you're right," he said quietly. "If I was Jimmy, I wouldn't be a big fan of me, either."

"George, it's not really that —"

"Bethy. Please."

"Well, okay. It's partly that," she said with a sigh. "He thinks you want me back."

George just smiled and didn't answer.

Beth looked down and tried to focus.

"So," she said.

"How does this work?" he asked. "Are we enemies again?"

"We were enemies?" she asked, startled.

"I wasn't your biggest fan right after we broke up," George admitted. "I might have cast you as a Public Enemy of George. Number One, even."

Beth frowned. "We weren't enemies, we were broken up," she told him. "And we're not enemies now. I think we need some space, that's all. It's like we only have two speeds: be together the way we always were, or don't speak at all. And we can't be together like we always were, so maybe we should take a step back."

"A non-talking, non-hanging-out step back," George said. He shrugged when she glared at him. "I'm just clarifying things."

"I don't think it's good for us to hold on," Beth said firmly. "I think you should date Larissa. You guys have so much in common, and you'll both be in Pittsburgh next year."

George blinked. "What?"

"I'm not saying you stopped dating her because of me, I'm just saying that it seems like maybe you did and if you did, maybe you should —"

"Beth." He interrupted her and then paused for a

moment, as if trying to calm down. "I get that you're over me, but you don't have to give me dating advice," he said.

And then the problem was what to say next. Beth knew there was nothing else to say, but she couldn't quite bring herself to just get up and walk away from him.

Not yet.

"Okay," she said eventually. "I guess I'm surprised that you're so understanding."

"Always," he replied with the ghost of his smile near his mouth. "Or almost always."

Beth looked at him then and it was like she fell into his eyes the way she used to, and could see their whole history spread out there. She remembered meeting him at that party when they were both freshmen. How he'd started talking to her and never once looked at her boobs, and that was back when Beth thought her boobs had taken over her life. Their marathon television-watching weekends, and numerous debates on who kicked more ass: Buffy or Aeryn Sun. Mini golf tournaments, George's birthday bonfires on the beach, their Halloween costumes . . . Even last year's hooker attire seemed almost funny now that she looked back on it. He was her entire high school experience, all wrapped up in one goofy, maddening, adorable guy.

She loved him, she knew in her heart. But she didn't want to be *in* love with him again. She didn't want the history and emotion that swirled all around them.

"Good-bye," Beth whispered.

"Take care, Bethy," George replied in a low voice, and he didn't look away.

She wanted to reach over and touch him, but she didn't.

Instead, she rose to her feet and tried not to cry as she turned away and marched toward her new life.

20

Kelsi sat on the front stoop of Bennett's building and let the hot city night settle all around her.

She wished she hadn't worn her favorite pair of jeans, because the August night was way too muggy for them. But when she'd made up her mind to head for New York City, it had been the middle of the night. The next morning, the alarm had gone off way too early, and Kelsi knew she should be grateful she'd managed to put her shirt on right side out.

It had been a long, stuffy car ride, and she'd rushed to Bennett's building filled to the brim with all the things she needed to say. It was a little bit of a letdown to have to wait.

Or maybe it was for the best, because the truth was, she wasn't sure what she had to say was even coherent.

Either way, she had nothing to do but sit and watch New Yorkers pass back and forth in front of her.

Skinny jeans were still in, if the girls sauntering by were any indication, which made Kelsi smile wryly. She would *never* wear skinny jeans. Her thighs were reasonably sized, which was why she didn't need to put them in jeans that would make a giraffe look fat.

She was giggling at that mental image when she saw Bennett come around the corner.

Her heart skipped a beat.

She was beginning to realize it always would, no matter what happened.

He looked simultaneously tired and keyed up, walking fast with his head down, his iPod in his ears. She knew the only exercise he got was walking, and he liked to do it to musical accompaniment. Kelsi was secretly glad, because she got to study him as he moved closer.

He was nearly on top of her before he noticed that there was someone sitting on his stoop, and it took a few moments for it to register that the person sitting there was Kelsi.

Bennett's entire face lit up.

On cue, Kelsi's heart melted.

"What are you doing? Where did you come from?" He was asking questions and chanting nonsense as he took her into his arms, rocking her back and forth and pressing kisses to her neck and the side of her face.

"Surprise!" She couldn't help but kiss him back. It was like she could never get enough of him. Kelsi tried to steel herself.

"This is fantastic!" Bennett continued happily, stepping back to look at her. "What's going on? I can't believe you didn't tell me you were coming down!"

Kelsi's smile faltered, and she reached over to stroke his jaw. Then she dropped her hand.

"We have to talk," she said.

Bennett frowned. He eased back a little bit, so he could search her face.

"No conversation that begins with that sentence leads anywhere I want to go," he said. "What do we have to talk about?"

Kelsi sucked in a breath, and then dove in.

"Your residency," she said.

Bennett looked at her, and then dropped his eyes.

"Taryn is dead," he muttered.

Kelsi shook her head. Her hurt feelings threatened to swamp her.

"Why are you keeping secrets from me?" she demanded. "First you didn't tell me you applied for the internship and now *this*? What's going on with you?"

Bennett sighed. "I guess I just didn't know what to say, so I didn't say anything."

"What relationship are *you* in?" Kelsi asked, suddenly

furious with him. "I thought we talked about everything! I thought that was the *point*."

"Everyone is so excited for me to be here," Bennett said after a moment, not meeting Kelsi's gaze. "But what if I'm not sure that this is the place for me? What if I'm not so sure I like it? How could I tell you that, when I know you think this is the best thing that ever happened to me?"

Kelsi processed that for a minute.

"You've changed here," she said, and it was such a relief to say it that she felt a warmth flood through her. She'd been waiting to say it for far too long.

"What do you mean?" he asked, frowning at her.

"I mean that you're different," Kelsi said. She laced her fingers together in front of her and concentrated on them fiercely. "When you started this job, you only pretended to be all snotty about art because that's what Carlos wanted to hear. But I don't think you're pretending anymore — I think part of you really is that New York hipster guy, full of himself and mean to other people." She looked at him then. "What happened to just loving art? Why do you have to judge everything?"

"I don't . . ." But whatever he'd been about to say, he didn't finish. "This is exactly what I'm talking about," he said instead. "I'm not so sure I like it here."

They sat quietly for a moment. Kelsi concentrated on the sound of traffic along the avenues.

"None of this even matters," Bennett said finally, taking Kelsi's hand. "I'm sorry I didn't tell you before, but it's irrelevant, anyway. I'm not taking the residency. I don't want to miss you this much."

"Missing me has nothing to do with it," Kelsi began.

"It has everything to do with it!" Bennett cried. "I mean, I don't know about becoming a New York hipster or whatever, but I know I want to be with you. This summer has sucked, Kels."

"I know," she said.

"See?" He slid his arms around her. "Settled." He rested his forehead against hers and breathed in. "How could I give this up, Kelsi? I'd have to be crazy."

"Bennett," she said, feeling brave and scared all at once. She took a breath and then let it out. "You have to take the residency. You know you do."

"It's too late," he said stubbornly.

Kelsi gently removed herself from his arms, and stood.

"It's not too late," she told him. "You have to think about what's best for you, Bennett. Take me out of the equation."

"You're what's best for me," he told her.

Kelsi looked at him, and she knew that she loved him more than she ever thought possible. She wanted nothing more than for the two of them to return to their schools and be together the way they been had last year.

But she also knew that wasn't the right thing for Bennett.

It was so strange to see things that way. To love him so much that she would prefer to see him doing what he was supposed to do — even if it meant losing him — rather than staying where they were just to hold on to him when it was clearly wrong.

"Kelsi?"

He looked so scared. Kelsi realized he thought she was going to end things, which was almost funny. She smiled at him instead.

"I love you," she told him. She felt strong and sad all at once.

"I love you, too," he said, still frozen in place.

"But you have to think about what's best for you, Bennett," Kelsi whispered. "We both do."

Ella let herself out the back door, letting it slap shut behind her. She had a bottle of Jägermeister she'd just liberated from her father's freezer and no clear idea about the best way to enjoy it.

It was coming up on six P.M. and she was bored. She went over the list of everyone who was off having fun without her: Jeremy was having an Almost End of the Summer event with his lifeguard buddies. Kelsi was still in New York, which was just as well, as thinking about her made Ella's stomach hurt. Taryn was nowhere to be found, which Ella assumed meant she was off with Peter, which also made Ella feel ill. Ella hadn't seen Beth all day. A large Tuttle contingent had taken a field trip to Bar Harbor, but Ella hadn't been able to force herself out of bed early enough to go with them.

That left Ella — and, apparently, one other cousin.

"It's you and me," Ella called to Jamie, who she could see lying down on one of the tabletops at the far end of the clearing. "Get ready to have fun, because I need you to amuse me."

As Ella drew closer, she saw that Jamie was on her cell phone. And that she was acting seventeen kinds of shady, too, whispering and muttering and hanging up before Ella could venture too close.

"Hi!" she cried, scrambling off the table and standing beside it. "I didn't know you were here!"

"Obviously," Ella said. She took in Jamie's flushed cheeks and the crazed look in her green eyes. "What's going on?"

"Oh, nothing," Jamie began in a completely over-the-top innocent voice.

"You're lying to me!" Ella cried, pretending to be shocked. Actually, she was thrilled. Intrigue! Her boredom disappeared at once. She shook her head at Jamie. "I definitely do not approve."

Ella flounced over and took a seat as if Jamie weren't behaving like a freak at all. She placed the bottle of Jäger in the middle of the table and waved at it.

"What?" Jamie looked at the bottle. "Oh. No, I don't want any."

"You need some," Ella told her firmly. "And then you

need to sit down and tell me why you've been acting so bizarre all summer."

"I've been acting bizarre?" Jamie asked. But she sat down. "You think so?"

"I think I saw more of you last summer when you were in a summer program a zillion miles away," Ella said mildly, reaching over and taking a swig. She shuddered. "I think you're hiding something, and you know how I get when I want to know a secret."

Jamie laughed. "I remember that time you forced me to tell you all about how I had a crush on Jon Tenenbaum, who was on my swim team at day camp," she said, her eyes lighting up with the memory. "I don't even know how you did it."

"I have magic powers," Ella drawled, pretending to wave an imaginary wand in the air.

"That's one way of looking at it," Jamie said with a snort.

"Don't think you're going to distract me," Ella warned Jamie. "All this memory lane stuff is fine, but I have a one-track mind."

"You used to," Jamie agreed. "Now instead of 'boys, boys, boys' it's 'Jeremy, Jeremy, Jeremy.'"

"That was a lame line," Ella told her sadly. "I'm not even a little bit distracted by that. I don't even think you could call that *trying* to distract me."

Jamie laughed again, and then reached over to help herself to the bottle of Jäger. Ella waited as Jamie took a healthy pull, and then laughed when Jamie made a disgusted face.

"Good for what ails you," Ella told her.

"It's disgusting," Jamie sputtered. "It tastes like medicine!"

"You stop tasting it after a while," Ella assured her. "Now stop talking about Jäger and tell me why, for the first time in your entire life, college is like this taboo subject for you."

Jamie tipped her head back toward the sky for a moment, and then looked over at Ella.

"I could," she said, "but I'm much more interested in what's going on with you."

"With me?" Ella shook her head. "Another pathetic attempt to divert attention away from yourself. *Nothing's* going on with me."

"Oh, yeah?" Her cousin's eyebrows rose. "So you don't have any issues with Taryn?"

"What?" Ella didn't like this turn of the conversation at all. "She's fine," she said carelessly. "If you like that sort of thing."

"Uh-huh." Jamie gave her a knowing look. "And you and Kelsi didn't have a big fight or anything, right?"

That was when Ella realized that Jamie had no intention of answering any of her questions.

She considered that for a moment, and thought that

really, she wasn't all that interested in answering Jamie's questions herself.

The cousins stared at each other for a long moment, with only the sounds of the distant waves between them, and then they both started giggling.

Ella raised the bottle between them in celebration of secrets left untold, and they both took another swig. Then they lay down on their respective sides of the table and waited for the stars to come out.

Looking at the sky, it took a while for them to notice a strange smell in the air.

"Hey," Jamie said, frowning. "Is that smoke?"

Ella sat up too quickly, and turned around. Smoke was pouring out of Beth's family's cottage in thick plumes, dark against the evening sky.

"Oh, my God," Ella cried, scrambling to her feet. "Is anyone in there?"

Beth leaned in to give Jimmy one last kiss and then smiled at him. They'd finished an early dinner and were drawing out their good-byes on the corner of Main Street.

Beth couldn't believe it, but summer was officially over. Baseball camp was finished for the season, and Jimmy was leaving Pebble Beach to head home for a week or so. He said that his parents had a place on the Jersey Shore where he'd stay before heading back to Bucknell for the fall semester.

What a strange summer, Beth thought, pulling away from Jimmy to look into his eyes.

"I'll call you as soon as I get home," Jimmy said. "And we'll e-mail."

"I know," Beth said, grinning. Beth thought that sounded

like fun, and imagined herself writing e-mails to Jimmy from her dorm room in Washington, DC.

"You're going to have an awesome time at Georgetown," Jimmy told her, as if reading her mind. "College sports are on a whole different plane than high school. Your level of competition is going to skyrocket."

"I'm really excited," Beth said. Then she couldn't contain herself any longer, and let her smile break loose. "Oh, and I got you something to remember the summer by!"

"You did?" Jimmy cocked his head a little bit to the side.

Beth laughed in delighted anticipation. "I saw it in a gift shop on Main Street the other day and I knew you had to have it," she told him. "It was obviously fate."

She reached into her bag and pulled out a plush stuffed pig. It looked like an exact replica of the one they'd seen at the baseball game, right down to the spots on its side.

With great flourish, Beth presented the pig to Jimmy. And then totally cracked up laughing, as the image of the real pig at the Portland Sea Dogs game raced through her mind.

"I was going to try to put a rake on its back," she told him through her giggles, "but it's really hard to find miniature rakes in Pebble Beach. Who knew?"

She laughed even harder and then wiped her eyes, and that's when she noticed that Jimmy wasn't laughing.

"What's wrong?" she asked.

Jimmy held the pig in his hands and looked at it like it was some kind of alien life-form. Like he'd never seen a stuffed animal before.

"Nothing's wrong," he said, staring down at it. He looked up at Beth. He was frowning slightly. "I just don't get it."

Beth blinked.

"It's supposed to be, like, the pig from the Sea Dogs game," she said. Jimmy looked at her, wearing a quizzical smile. "You know, the one that raked the infield during the seventh inning stretch?"

Did he really not remember?

"Okay," he said, sounding confused. "But what am I supposed to do with it?"

By this point, Beth just felt kind of embarrassed about the whole thing.

"You're not supposed to *do* anything with it, Jimmy," she said. She gestured at the pig sort of helplessly. "I mean . . . it's a *pig*."

Jimmy looked at the pig, and then he looked at Beth.

"Thanks," he said, but Beth could tell that he was just saying it out of politeness. He really didn't understand why she'd given it to him.

"It's just funny," Beth tried again.

And as Jimmy looked at the pig again, as if he was waiting for it to explain Beth's behavior to him, Beth had the most unsettling thought.

Didn't Jimmy have a sense of humor?

Because as they stood there both staring at the stupid stuffed pig, Beth couldn't remember a single time when Jimmy had actually laughed about anything. Smiled, sure, but laughed?

And had he ever made *her* laugh?

She racked her brain. When they'd been at the baseball game, Beth had laughed so hard when the pig came out but Jimmy hadn't, now that she thought of it. At the time, she'd figured that he had just been really into the game, so he'd ignored the hysterical thing happening. And then later, it hadn't been an issue because he'd wanted to kiss her so badly.

But what if that wasn't it at all? What if he just didn't get why a pig with rake on its back was funny? Because Beth thought that something so over-the-top was something you either found hysterical or you didn't, and no amount of explaining would make any difference.

She and Jimmy said their good-byes, promised to keep in touch, and kissed again.

It was a long, sweet kiss, and Beth definitely enjoyed the touch of his mouth on hers, but something had changed. Her heart didn't pound the way it had before.

"I'm going to miss you," Jimmy told her.

"Same," Beth whispered, but she felt like she was lying somehow.

She watched him walk away from her, down Main Street and past the pier toward the car he'd loaded up with all his stuff from the summer. Then she tucked her hands into the pockets of her new American Eagle jeans and started her walk toward home.

She couldn't believe what had just happened. More than that, she couldn't believe she'd hung out with this guy all summer and hadn't noticed his humor deficit. How was that possible?

The thing was, Jimmy was so athletic, and that made him so different from the other guys she'd known. Now that she thought about it, that was pretty much all that they'd talked about: sports. It had been a lot of fun for Beth to talk so much about that part of her life, but there was more to her than just athletics.

As she headed inland toward the road that led back toward her family's cottages, Beth wondered if maybe she'd been paying too much attention to the *idea* of moving on. Because Jimmy was the first guy she'd noticed at all since she and George had broken up.

Maybe noticing him had just been a way for her to figure out that she *could* notice a guy. It didn't necessarily mean that she was destined to fall in love with him or anything.

And maybe she didn't want to be with a guy who didn't get why that pig was funny, after all. Maybe Jimmy was that other kind of summer boy — the kind you stopped thinking about as soon as the weather turned colder.

Beth was so lost in thought that she didn't notice the first fire truck that zoomed past.

It was the second one, or maybe the third, that caught her attention.

She looked up, and that was when she saw the smoke. It billowed up from the trees in front of her — the trees that, she knew, surrounded her family's little compound. The smoke was so dark that it was almost black against the sky, and it made absolutely no sense.

Beth knew what smoke meant. Everyone knew what smoke meant.

It was like her brain completely froze, and then reset.

Beth didn't even think. She just broke into a run.

Beth had run that same stretch a thousand times.

During the school year, she sometimes even imagined running it while she was inside on the treadmill, because it was so beautiful, the way the dirt road curved into the dark woods, like it was curving into someplace magical. The mossy smells and deep pine usually embraced her, soothed her.

Not tonight.

Beth pumped her legs and her arms, her throat burning. Burning. She wasn't aware of breathing and when she made it around that last, final bend, she skidded to a stop.

The fire trucks were pulled up into the clearing, and firefighters in their yellow coveralls marched here and there with their hats pulled tight on their foreheads. Smoke still rose behind them. A hose poured water, and men shouted to each other in thick Maine accents. Beth could see all that.

But it was what was behind them that Beth couldn't make sense of.

Her house was gone.

The walls still stood, but they were blackened, and bits of roof were clinging to the charred remains. Everything else was just . . . rubble.

She bent over to put her hands on her knees, gasping for air, as frantic, panicked thoughts of her family filled her mind.

"Beth!"

She heard her name, but couldn't move. Suddenly, her mother was crying at her side, and she folded Beth into her arms.

"Oh, thank God!" she cried.

Next to her, Beth's father looked ghostly pale. "We didn't know where you were, kiddo," he said gruffly, and pulled her into a hug of his own.

Beth was just thankful they were okay. Her mind reeled away from thinking that through. From picturing what them *not* being okay might have been like. It was paralyzing.

"Is everyone . . . ?" She was afraid to ask.

And then she didn't have to.

She found herself swept up by all of her cousins at once. Ella grabbed her around the neck and Jamie bear-hugged the both of them. The rest of the Tuttles came to stand around them in a small, quiet circle, as if they were trying to figure out together what was happening.

For a long time, Beth just stood and watched, dazed on such a deep level that she didn't notice the tears pouring down her face until they tickled her neck.

Behind them, a car pulled into the driveway, sweeping everything with its headlights. In the twin beams, Beth saw that there was nothing identifiable in the mess of blackened rubble. Everything was just . . . gone.

Kelsi came racing over, her eyes wide with panic, and when she saw Beth and her parents standing there, whole and sound, she burst into tears.

"What happened?" Kelsi demanded through her sobs.

But all Beth could think was: *Everything is gone.*

Her whole childhood. All those summers. She had known every single floorboard in that back bedroom she'd slept in. She knew every settling sound the little cottage made during the night. She could walk through the entire place blindfolded and barefoot. Sometimes during the cold, bleak Massachusetts winters, she would dream that she was back in her Maine bedroom, and would dream of waking up and fixing breakfast, then settling in the front room that caught the morning light. She couldn't believe that she would never sit on that couch again, or look out the tiny porthole window in the bathroom.

She had so many memories of the cottage that she couldn't accept that it had just disappeared while she was off having dinner. How could that be?

"It was the lint trap," Beth's mother was telling Kelsi. "In the dryer. The fireman told me it's fairly common. We're just lucky no one was hurt, and that the fire was contained in the one cottage. When you think what might have happened . . ." But she didn't finish.

Beth watched her father wrap his arm around her mother's shoulders.

Beth had never really thought about the fact that fire trucks were always racing to specific fires. Or the fact that fires could do this — reduce a whole lifetime of memories to ash.

She'd lost her virginity in that cottage just last summer. It had seemed so perfect because the summer before, also right here, she'd realized how in love she was with George.

She'd become who she was here, and now she didn't know what that meant. If her childhood was gone in a flash like this . . . if everything could change so horribly, so suddenly . . .

"Beth."

She knew that voice, and turned, not at all surprised that he was there.

What *was* surprising was that George was covered in soot. His hair was even wilder than usual.

"What happened?" she demanded, not realizing it was the first she'd spoken until she heard her own cracked voice. "Are you hurt?"

"No," George said, his own voice scratchy. "I saw the smoke. No one knew where you were." His dark eyes locked on to hers.

"I was in town," Beth whispered. "I was having dinner with Jimmy."

"Thank God for Jimmy Neutron," George said brokenly, and he even smiled. Then he reached into his pocket. "Here."

"What is it?" she asked, because his hand was still a fist.

"I found it in the —" George stopped, and his throat worked, as if it hurt to swallow. "I don't know why it wasn't burned."

He opened his hand.

It was the cork fisherman figurine that had once sat on the shelf above the light switch in Beth's bedroom. It was slightly blackened at the edges, but still, unmistakably, it was the same silly knickknack that George had named Chauncey.

Beth had never been so glad to see Chauncey's silly little

shape in her life. She grabbed it and smiled before putting it in her pocket. She felt more tears fill her eyes.

"I'm glad you're okay," George said quietly, and he smiled.

Beth watched him start to walk away, but it was like she saw it from a distance. She saw the remains of her cottage, and wondered, suddenly, what she was supposed to take from this.

She'd been so afraid of the way that her life was changing that she'd clung to a friendship with George, as if that could stall it. But the moment she'd suspected that maybe they could work their way back to what they'd been, she'd recoiled. Because she didn't want to go backward, she'd told herself. She wanted to go forward into her new life. And whatever else George was, he wasn't new.

But he was so much else.

She didn't want to be in love with him because it was complicated. They'd broken up for a lot of valid reasons. Loving him hurt. Beth had wanted a fresh start because it was easier.

But she thought that maybe, while the firefighters were trudging through the remains of her house, *easy* wasn't exactly in the cards anymore.

Not after tonight.

She pulled the little cork figurine back out of her pocket.

And as she held the remains of Chauncey in her palms, she knew two things. That she could make all the plans she wanted, but those didn't much matter when fate stepped in.

And that memories were more precious than she ever could have imagined — and sometimes, it turned out they were all that anyone had left.

24

Ella scurried into the room with a huge mountain of clothes obscuring her face.

"Are we doing laundry?" Jamie asked from where she was lounging across the farthest of the twin beds. Next to her, Beth snickered. The fact that she could laugh made everyone else relax a little bit.

The whole family was still in a state of shock. Beth's parents were bunking down on Ella's pullout couch, while the cousins and Taryn were having an impromptu sleepover in Kelsi's room. It felt bizarre, Kelsi thought, to be having an all-cousin sleepover party under such terrible circumstances.

Without discussing it, Kelsi had pulled the shades down on the windows that looked out over the remains of Beth's cottage. They'd all stared at it enough tonight.

"I don't do laundry," Ella said then, tipping her pile forward so that all her clothes fell onto the edge of the other bed, where Kelsi and Taryn were sitting cross-legged. "These are for Beth."

Everyone stared at the clothes, a riot of color that spilled across the coverlet. They'd all contributed from their own wardrobes. Beth was wearing a pair of Kelsi's sweats with one of Jamie's huge, blanket-like sweaters. She'd taken a very long, very hot shower and Kelsi had heard her crying softly under the spray. Now her eyes were red, but her skin was scrubbed clean and her flaxen hair was in a damp ponytail high on her head.

Kelsi thought Beth looked older somehow. She felt that way herself. Like everything had changed, in ways she couldn't even imagine just yet. She shook the feeling off.

"At least it was just the summer cottage," Jamie said softly, patting Beth's leg. "If it had been your house in Martin . . ."

Beth scooted off the edge of the bed and picked up one of the items of clothing Ella had brought. It was a tiny little tank top with the words TEAM JOLIE emblazoned across the front. It looked like it would barely fit Ella, much less Beth.

"If I didn't know better," Beth said drily, "I would think you set the fire yourself, El, so that I'd be forced to wear your clothes. After so many years of trying to get me into them."

Ella stuck her tongue out at Beth and flopped down on the chair in the corner of the room.

"Not to mention," Beth continued with that same dry, sort of dark tone. "I am totally Team Aniston."

"Of course you are," Ella said with a dramatic eye roll. "Big surprise there."

There was no real laughter, not yet. But it felt good to be all together, safe and sound despite the fire.

"What a night," Kelsi sighed, leaning back against the headboard. Next to her, Taryn smiled at her for the first time in what felt like ages. Kelsi guessed the fire had scared everybody into being nicer.

"I have a confession to make," Jamie announced into the quiet.

"About time," Ella murmured. Jamie glanced at her.

"Ella told me earlier tonight that she thought I was acting weird this summer, and it's true." Jamie took a deep breath. "I know I've been strange."

"Yeah," Beth said, turning to look at Jamie. "Like when you abandoned me before we were supposed to go dorm room shopping."

"Or when you refused to talk about hanging out in Northampton with us," Kelsi agreed, exchanging a look with Taryn.

Jamie looked up at the painted white ceiling with the cracks running through it, and then back at her cousins.

"I don't know why I didn't tell anyone," she said in a small voice. "I kind of didn't want people to freak out or anything."

"You can tell us anything," Kelsi assured her. "Nobody's going to freak out." After the fire, any other kind of freak-out seemed minor.

"Seriously," Beth agreed. "We're family."

Jamie raised her shoulders up and then spit it out, like she was afraid of losing her nerve. "There was this guy last summer, at the writing program," she said. "We were buddies. It was great. And then we e-mailed all year."

"Is this a friends to more-than-friends thing?" Ella asked. "Because I think Beth could give you some pointers on that one." She considered. "Or, you know, maybe not."

"Shut up, Ella," Beth said mildly.

"Go on," Kelsi urged Jamie.

"There was this reunion thing we had over spring break," Jamie continued, a bit dreamily. "Dex and I had broken up, and there was just something about Mark. It was like I'd never seen him before. We totally got together."

"Define *together*," Ella suggested, with a wicked grin.

"None of your business, gutter brain," Jamie replied tartly.

"Everyone knows what it means when people say 'none of your business,'" Ella murmured, arching her brows at everyone except Jamie.

"Can she tell her story?" Kelsi asked Ella. The sisters looked at each other for a moment. Ella had grabbed on and hugged Kelsi tight when her sister had arrived at the scene of the fire, but Kelsi was all too aware that they still hadn't talked since their big fight. Things were still unresolved between them. She wasn't surprised when Ella looked away.

"Anyway, we ended up seeing a lot of each other since then," Jamie was saying, blushing.

"I don't get the need for secrecy," Beth said. "Since when have we *not* been excited about you getting together with a boy?"

"We already know you met him at voluntary summer school, so I think the dork factor is already out of the bag," Ella said as if she was agreeing with Beth. She gave Jamie a lazy smile. "No need to hide it."

"You're hilarious," Jamie told her. She wrinkled her nose. "The thing is, Mark is deferring Amherst for a year. He was supposed to start with me this fall, but he wants to backpack around Europe instead. See the world. Get a little perspective." Jamie looked down, focusing on the silver rings on her fingers. "Do you know that I've been so focused on getting into Amherst that it, like, took over my whole life?"

The others all looked at one another, amused. Ella tried to muffle her snorty laugh. Beth laughed without hiding it.

"Um, yes," Kelsi said when no one else spoke. "We know."

Jamie looked up, and her green eyes were filled with something Kelsi had never seen in them before. Jamie had always been driven. But this was a different kind of ambition altogether.

"I'm going with him," she whispered. "I'm postponing school for a year. I'm just going to see what happens. It's so unlike me that it's been keeping me up at night, but it's the exact right thing to do. I know it." Jamie let out a breath, and gave a small smile. "Surprise," she added softly.

There was a beat of silence.

"Wow!" Kelsi breathed. It was more than a surprise. For studious Jamie, it was like a revolution.

"That sounds amazing," Taryn said firmly.

Beth shook her head. "Did your parents freak?"

"They were surprisingly okay with it," Jamie said, looking still taken aback by that unexpected turn. "But I was much more worried about telling you guys." She looked at Kelsi specifically. "I thought you'd give me a hard time, for sure."

"Me? Why?" Kelsi asked. "Are you kidding? I'd love to go to Europe!"

"Kelsi's not *all* about academics the way she used to be," Ella said, and giggled. "That's what happens when you get a life." She still didn't look at Kelsi, but Kelsi thought that it sounded a lot more affectionate than it could have. She chose to take it as a good sign.

"I thought everyone would think I'm crazy," Jamie said softly. "I've been obsessed with Amherst since I was a kid. All I've ever wanted was to go there. And now I'm putting it off a year?"

"Well," Beth said philosophically, "you were there all last summer. Maybe that eased your obsession a little bit."

"You don't think I'm crazy?" Jamie asked.

"No!" everybody cried — everybody except Ella.

"I think you're completely crazy," Ella said when everyone else fell quiet, "for not telling me so we could plan the perfect European wardrobe. But other than that, no way. I think you're going to have the most incredible time!"

"Me, too!" Jamie whispered, her green eyes glowing. "I'm so excited!"

Kelsi's phone buzzed then, and she picked it up to see that it was Bennett.

"I have to take this," she told the girls, and jumped to her feet.

Out on the back steps, Kelsi sat with her knees pulled up, hunched over against the chill of the night air. It still smelled like fire, even though there was a fairly decent breeze. Fire and yet mixed with the normal smells of Maine: sea, pine, and the hint of moss and deep greens from the woods. Far above, the moon shone down as if nothing had happened.

Kelsi filled Bennett in on the whole story, wishing all the time that he was there to give her the hug she so desperately needed. Even with the tense way they'd left things, she still believed that everything was better when he was near. It felt good to know that.

"I'm so glad everyone's okay," Bennett said quietly. "I mean, it could have happened in the middle of the night. I can't even think about it."

"We're really lucky, I guess," Kelsi said. It sounded strange to say that out loud. Beth and her parents had lost so much. So much of what made summer summer. The entire Tuttle family was changed by what had happened that night. And yet, they were so very, very lucky.

"What about us, Kelsi?" Bennett asked softly. "Are we okay?"

"I don't know." Kelsi thought her voice sounded loud in the night. "I hope so." She closed her eyes. "Have you decided what you're going to do?"

Bennett sighed.

"It's hard," he said. "I mean, I know you're right. I know I should take it. I just can't get my head around not being with you."

"Then it sounds to me like you've decided," Kelsi said. She sort of wished someone was witnessing this. She was being so brave. Everyone talked about loving someone and setting them free, but who really did it?

"I know that this could be the best thing that ever happened to me," Bennett said, his voice thickening. "I know I'd have to be crazy not to do it."

"I think," Kelsi said, "that you would regret it for the rest of your life."

"We'll just make it work," Bennett said then. "I mean, we have to. I can't do this without you, Kels. It's like I can feel myself turning into an asshole and you're the only thing that keeps me grounded. You keep me *me*."

"I want us to work, too," Kelsi told him then. "I think we can do it. I really do."

"I bet every couple says that," Bennett pointed out. "And yet no one seems to know of a long-distance relationship that lasts."

"I know of a long-distance relationship that worked," Kelsi said after a minute. "That's working right now, in fact. My sister's. They had some rocky times, but they're fine now. Great, even." She smiled, thinking of Ella and how much she'd changed in the past two years. "And believe me, she would have once told you long distance was impossible — and that's when she thought the term meant a guy who didn't happen to be right in front of her that very second."

"Well, if Ella can do it," Bennett said, with a laugh in his voice, "then I think we should be able to."

Kelsi didn't know what would happen in the coming

year. But she did know one thing: She wouldn't have changed a single thing that brought her to this point.

"I have a good feeling," she told him then.

"Oh, yeah?" She could hear him smiling.

"Yeah," she said. She was smiling, too, as if he were in front of her. As if she could reach out and take his hand. "I waited my whole life for you. Now that I've found you, what's a little commute?"

The back door opened, and Ella jerked upright, whirling around from the open refrigerator door.

"My God," she said when her heart stopped pounding, "you scared me to death."

Kelsi stood there, looking cold in her pajama bottoms and a Smith sweatshirt, her cheeks flushed pink. She held her cell phone in her hand, and Ella didn't even know why she'd been so startled: She'd known Kelsi had gone off to take a phone call.

Staring at her sister in the pale fluorescent light in the kitchen, Ella marveled at how much had changed over the past two years. And in a weird way, Peter was to thank for a lot of it. He was why Ella had felt so guilty and had gone out of her way to be good to Kelsi two years ago. He was why Ella and Kelsi had had that huge blowup last summer, which had been awful at the time, but which Ella thought had brought them even closer.

And he was responsible once again for what Ella had learned most recently: that it didn't matter who Kelsi felt closer to — she and Ella were sisters, and that was just deeper. Ella had done some bad things to Kelsi over the years. If it were Kelsi's turn to be a little less loving, well, Ella would just have to suck it up.

The phrasing of that was vintage Jeremy, of course, but the sentiment was true either way.

She didn't realize that the moment had stretched out until Kelsi spoke into the silence between them.

"Okay," Kelsi said, nodding. "You're mad at me. I guess that's understandable. I should have realized how upset you were."

Ella stood up a little straighter, and found herself noticing random things, like the new wind chimes one of her aunts must have hung near the hammock, and the low tones the brass tubes sent spilling across the clearing outside and into the open windows, lulling them all into a false sense of security.

She also noticed that Kelsi wasn't exactly apologizing.

Part of her wanted an apology. She'd been hurt, and she wanted Kelsi to acknowledge that — to feel guilty about it.

But if how angry she'd been about Taryn and Peter was any indication of how she'd felt about *herself* and Peter (which was what Jeremy kept saying), then maybe the fact that Kelsi couldn't make her feel better was related to everything that had happened over the last few summers.

Ella still didn't know why Kelsi had forgiven her for sleeping with Peter.

But she could, in a small way, return the favor.

"I'm not upset," she said, looking at her older sister. "I was, but I'm fine. You, however, look kind of sad. I mean more than we all do tonight."

Kelsi sighed and shrugged.

"It's Bennett," she said, and then she walked past Ella to collapse onto one of the kitchen chairs and let the whole story spill out.

How Bennett hadn't even told her about his decision and just pretended everything was fine when they talked, no matter how much she'd pushed. How Taryn had been so furious with her, and had spent the week of rain only speaking to Kelsi if it related directly to the *Buffy* episode they were watching. How Kelsi had confronted Bennett, and how they'd decided that he would take the internship.

"Which means we won't be together," Kelsi said softly.

"Why can't you be together?" Ella demanded, readjusting herself in the chair across from Kelsi.

"We can be together long-distance," Kelsi said, "but that's not the same as being together every day. We'll have to adapt."

"True. It's all ticking clocks and having to leave," Ella said, thinking of the year ahead. She didn't really want to confront going back to that place with Jeremy. It was so much better when they could see each other all the time — when phone and e-mail weren't their major forms of interaction. But Ella couldn't let herself think too much about it tonight. She would get way too sad.

But it was kind of nice to share a knowing sort of smile with her sister, because now they both understood how hard long-distance love *was*.

"The worst part," Kelsi confessed after a moment, "is that there's a really big part of me that wishes Taryn hadn't told me what was happening. I kind of want to ignore it, so we can just all go back to school and be together again."

"It's okay to be a little mad at her," Ella said. "It really wasn't any of her business."

"I know you don't like her," Kelsi said, looking up at her sister. She shrugged. "I just don't know *why* you don't. I thought you guys would love each other."

Ella chose not to dig into that statement, which clearly indicated that Taryn didn't like Ella very much, either.

"It's not that I don't like her." Ella leaned forward so she could be direct. "It's that . . . she wears the same bikini I do, in, like, the same exact way."

Kelsi blinked. "What?"

Ella raised one shoulder. "You know. If *you* wore the same bikini as me, there would be a whole different vibe. I like being the only person who wears *my* black bikini in *my* way." She hoped she was explaining herself.

Kelsi actually laughed. "I kind of see your point," she said.

"And I think that you can grow to tolerate and even appreciate someone who wears the same bikini," Ella said, slowly, "but you're never going to be BFF. You know?"

"I do know," Kelsi said. Her brown eyes were warm when she looked over. "Just for the record, I only have one sister."

Ella made a face, to hide the fact that she was ridiculously touched by Kelsi's words. "I know how many sisters you have," she assured her. "Believe me."

"Okay, then," Kelsi said. "Just so we're clear."

Ella could sense a difference in the air — an easing. The summer was over, Ella thought, and somehow she and Kelsi had found their way back to each other. She would try to remember that they always did.

"So," she said casually. She smirked slightly and raised her eyebrows at Kelsi. "You've had sex."

Kelsi flushed, and then shrugged. "It's true," she said. "I have."

Ella could see the traces of wariness in her sister's gaze. She felt a surge of protectiveness and love. She propped her chin on her hand and raised her brows.

"I don't know what you're waiting for," she said lightly. "Tell me everything."

The next morning, Beth woke up very early, jolting awake at her normal running time. She blinked in surprise to find herself trapped in a too-small bright blue sleeping bag she recognized as her aunt's from, like, the seventies. She was also crammed into a corner of Kelsi's floor between a gently snoring Ella and the wall.

First, she remembered Jimmy and the stuffed pig incident, and wondered again if she should keep in touch with him. She didn't know how to go about processing that.

Then she thought about going for a run on her own this morning, since she was awake — and that was when she remembered the night before.

And next she remembered that she no longer had running shoes. Then everything else hit her. It was dizzying.

Beth crawled out of her little sleeping area, and shivered the moment her warm skin encountered the cold morning air. It was already getting chillier, and any day now there might even be frost on the ground despite the summer sun in the sky. Autumn came so much quicker in Maine.

Beth snuck over to the window shade that Kelsi had shut the night before, and pulled up a corner of it so she could let herself peek out. Part of her truly expected the fire to have been some kind of horrific nightmare. She would peel back the shade and see the cottage standing where it had always —

But no, the nightmare was real.

Beth inhaled a deep, shaky breath as she looked at the pile of charred rubble that stood where the cottage should have been. The first morning light was just sneaking into the clearing, illuminating the dew on the grass and the sickening wreck of Beth's summers, which were now just so much dark ash.

Beth decided to crawl back into her sleeping bag, and pull the covers over her head. She couldn't cry, exactly, but she let the heaviness weigh on her until she drifted back to sleep.

Later that morning, all the girls woke up together when Ella and Kelsi's dad appeared in the doorway.

"Time to get moving, ladies," he announced, making Ella groan from beneath her pillow.

And so the Tuttles set about packing up the summer a

whole week early. Beth didn't like the idea of summer ending, but there was no use arguing about it. Beth's family's
cottage was gone, and all the Tuttles were leaving Maine
so that the landlord could decide what to do with the
property.

Beth spent the first part of the morning realizing, as she
observed the beautiful sunlight that illuminated the blackened remains of her cottage, that unlike her cousins, she had
nothing to pack up. Talk about traveling light. She pulled
on the jeans she'd been wearing the night before, and a
T-shirt of Kelsi's that had Janis Joplin on the front, and that
was pretty much that.

At first she tried to make jokes about it, because she was
getting in the way while her cousins wrestled clothes into
duffel bags and gathered up towels and shampoo and the
shoes they hadn't worn since they arrived in June.

But it became a whole lot less funny the longer it went
on, and Beth wandered out to the clearing to look at what
was left. Her Uncle Carr was making trip after trip to his
Jetta, packing boxes and bags, and he stopped when he saw
Beth standing there.

"Are you okay?" he asked.

"I think so," Beth said, and smiled so he'd believe it. But
inside, she wasn't sure. She was fine, of course. But she
didn't think she was the same.

And it made Beth's heart hurt.

So she walked down to the beach, where she could look at the ocean. She whispered her final good-bye to the water, the way she did every year, and hated that this time it felt so much more final.

Everything changes, she told herself. The trick was to concentrate on the good things. Like how lucky she was to even be here, looking at the ocean. It could all have been so much worse. She'd only lost *things.*

Things could be replaced. It was people Beth knew she couldn't do without. And she knew that to be true this morning in ways she couldn't have imagined the night before.

After standing with her feet in the sand for a long time, she slid her flip-flops back on and walked back to the cottages to find her cousins sitting together in the clearing.

"There you are," Ella said. "We were waiting for you."

Beth slid onto the picnic table next to her, and the four Tuttle girls sat there in the quiet of the late morning, listening to the chimes in the wind and looking at the great mess of Beth's cottage in front of them.

"What a weird summer," Jamie said after a while, in a small, almost wistful voice.

"I think it's going to be fine." Ella's voice was very sure. "I'm sure they'll build a new cottage, right?"

"Even if they rebuild it, it won't be the same," Beth said then, with a sigh. "They can't replace the board in the kitchen where my mom recorded our heights. Or the secret place in the headboard of the bed in my bedroom. They can't bring it back."

"But on the upside," Ella said with a wink, "they might install a shower with actual pressure, so you don't have to keep using ours."

"That's what I love about you," Beth replied with an eye roll. "Always practical."

There was a long, quiet moment then. Seagulls wheeled in lazy circles far overhead, and the sun seemed sharp. Beth felt an ache in her chest, like crying, although she wasn't. Not yet.

Next to her, Ella made a small noise. "You guys," she said, as if she was trying to convince herself along with everyone else, "there will always be other summers. This one is just ending a little soon. That's all."

There was another small silence. Beth flexed her toes against the soles of her flip-flops and kept her eyes on the burned-down cottage. This felt like a bigger ending to her than just the last day of summer.

"I don't know," Kelsi said after a moment. She looked quickly at Ella, then at the pine needles carpeting the ground below her. "I'm not sure I'll come up for the whole summer next year. Driving back and forth to the city wasn't fun at all. If things work out with Bennett, I think I'll probably just stay there with him."

"I don't think I'll be back by next summer, either," Jamie

chimed in with a guilty shrug of her shoulders. "Mark and I want to travel as long as possible. And then we'll have to deal with culture shock and stuff before we go to school."

"It's nuts," Beth said then, still staring at the burnt remains of her cottage. "I can't imagine coming here and *not* staying in that cottage. A replacement cottage might be too much for me. Too depressing."

"I've never heard such a load of crap in my life," Ella scolded them, her voice outraged now. "This is Pebble Beach. This is where we come in the summer. *I* will be here with a smile on my face just as soon as I get the hell out of high school next summer. And I fully expect you to be here, too. Every summer. *Hello!*"

Kelsi rolled her eyes at her little sister, but her smile was affectionate. "You say that now, but just you wait," she warned.

"I'm not talking about this anymore with any of you. You're officially in trouble." Ella glared at each of them in turn. "You can't just abandon Pebble Beach!"

"Your boyfriend is three minutes away," Kelsi pointed out. "If that changes, you might change your mind."

"Things do change, El," Jamie agreed, grinning. "Look at me. Look at you."

"We are Tuttles. We belong in Pebble Beach," Ella said very deliberately. When Beth opened her mouth to speak, she waved her hand at her. "I don't want to hear any more! This is blasphemy!"

Ella jumped off the table and, with another glare at everyone, turned on her heel and flounced toward her sunporch. Laughing, Kelsi and Jamie followed her.

But Beth stayed put.

She drew in a breath. The usual golden sunshine and pine smell was tainted with the smell of the fire, but she knew that wouldn't last forever. Next summer, the woods would smell the way they were supposed to. The sun would be bright, the sky would stretch blue and clear above the green trees, and the water would smack against the shore.

It made her feel better to think of it that way, no matter where she might be at this time next year.

Beth stood in the dirt driveway to wave everybody off, which felt strange. Normally, Uncle Carr's family was the last to go.

"We'll see you at Thanksgiving," Kelsi said, giving Beth a huge hug. Then she climbed into her car, where Taryn was already picking through CDs in the passenger seat.

"I'm going to have to do the college-visit thing this fall," Ella reminded Beth with a knowing sort of look. "So, obviously, I'll have to hit D.C. and we'll party."

"Anytime," Beth said.

Ella got into the backseat, and leaned over the seat divider to give Kelsi bossy directions to Jeremy's house.

"I know where he lives!" Kelsi snapped, and then the sisters made faces at each other.

Beth smiled and waved as they drove away.

She helped her aunts and uncles cram the last tennis rackets and wet bathing suits into their cars, and then hugged Jamie tight after she'd stowed away her backpack.

"You better keep in touch," Beth told her fiercely.

"I'm going to keep a blog," Jamie promised. "I swear. It'll be like I'm just away at school."

"I'll see you," Beth said softly.

And then her cousins were all gone and she was alone. The clearing felt empty without them, and so did Beth. And then she knew what she had to do.

While her parents sat down with the fire inspectors, Beth took her last walk of the summer.

She walked down the dirt road, and turned onto the coast road. She followed it all the way into town and stopped for a moment to watch the summer crowds on the pier. Out in the water, the rocky islands glittered in the sunlight, and far above, birds made lazy circles around and around before landing in the upper branches of the tall pines.

Taking a deep breath of the salty air, Beth turned away from the water and followed the street that wound a bit inland, passing the town library where Beth and her cousins had spent many a rainy afternoon when they were kids. She found her way past cottages with bright flower boxes at the windows and bright white picket fences. She stopped at the farthest one before the woods and went around the house to the back.

George was packing up his car in the driveway behind the little house. When Beth came down the drive, he turned, looking surprised.

"Are you all right?" he asked. He closed the distance between them, his hands going out automatically and catching her shoulders.

For a moment, she couldn't breathe.

And just like that, Beth knew.

A warmth of certainty rushed through her.

"I lost so much last night," she told him in a rush. "I can't lose you, too."

George stared at her for a long moment, and Beth thought she could see the fire reflected in his eyes. But that didn't make any sense. The fire had been out for a long time now.

It was her whole life hanging here, Beth thought, waiting for him to respond. Waiting for him, the way she thought she might always be. The way Jimmy thought George had been waiting himself.

He wasn't just a guy, an ex. He was George. He was part of her.

"You have me, Bethy," he said softly. "And you'll always have me."

A tidal wave of emotion swept over Beth, and she caved. She barely felt George's arms as they went around her, barely heard whatever soothing things he whispered in her ear.

But she knew he was there.

And it meant everything.

After a while, Beth realized that he was holding her close, and she tipped her head up to look him in the eye. She loved the way his arms fit so perfectly around her. How their mouths were so close, almost touching, at the perfect angle. She loved that spark deep in his eyes, and she loved that she didn't care what happened next. She just wanted to keep holding on to him.

Beth tilted her head up, and kissed him.

He felt new and wonderful, and like coming home.

The kiss was so sweet she felt tears crowd her eyes. She didn't know what it meant — she was going to Georgetown and he was going to Pitt. They couldn't really get back together now. She wasn't sure she even wanted to. But something was there that they couldn't deny. It would always be there. They both sighed, and then smiled at each other.

"I should go," she told him, her smile fading. "My parents are waiting, and I just wanted to say good-bye."

"It's not good-bye, Bethy. Not for good." He touched her face and for a moment, she held his hand and looked in his eyes. There was so much history there, so much warmth and friendship and hope. Beth knew that no matter what, George would always be a part of her life.

"Bye, George," Beth said, softly. She turned back up the drive, willing herself not to cry. As she walked through the shady pines, taking in her last deep breaths of the clean Maine air, Beth thought about George and about everything that had happened this summer.

In a way, Beth *had* lost everything. But as she took one last look at Dean packing up the car, she suddenly realized that there was a lot more to these summers in Maine than just, well, being in Maine.

For a few brief, glorious weeks, everyone important to her set aside the rest of their lives — work, stress, school — and just cared about one another. Beth realized that even if her family lost everything, they would still have one another and they would all still have that feeling of Maine. And she now knew that George was somehow included in that wonderful, unconditional pact.

Beth smiled as the sunlight broke through the trees and onto her face. She knew that she was moving on to her future. But that didn't mean that she had to leave anything — or anyone — behind.

To Do List: Read all the Point books!

By Aimee Friedman

☐ **South Beach**
0-439-70678-5

☐ **French Kiss**
0-439-79281-9

☐ **Hollywood Hills**
0-439-79282-7

By Hailey Abbott

☐ **Summer Boys**
0-439-54020-8

☐ **Next Summer: A Summer Boys Novel**
0-439-75540-9

☐ **After Summer: A Summer Boys Novel**
0-439-86367-8

☐ **Last Summer: A Summer Boys Novel**
0-439-86725-8

By Claudia Gabel

☐ **In or Out**
0-439-91853-7

By Nina Malkin

☐ **6X: The Uncensored Confessions**
0-439-72421-X

☐ **6X: Loud, Fast, & Out of Control**
0-439-72422-8

☐ **Orange Is the New Pink**
0-439-89965-6

POINTCKLT

I ♥ Bikinis series

❏ I ♥ Bikinis:
He's with Me
By Tamara Summers
0-439-91850-2

❏ I ♥ Bikinis:
Island Summer
By Jeanine Le Ny
0-439-91851-0

❏ I ♥ Bikinis:
What's Hot
By Caitlyn Davis
0-439-91852-9

By Erin Haft

❏ Pool Boys
0-439-83523-2

By Laura Dower

❏ Rewind
0-439-70340-9

By Jade Parker

❏ To Catch a Pirate
0-439-02694-6

By Randi Reisfeld and H.B. Gilmour

❏ Oh Baby!
0-439-67705-X

Story Collections

❏ Fireworks: Four
Summer Stories
By Niki Burnham, Erin
Haft, Sarah Mlynowski,
and Lauren Myracle
0-439-90300-9

❏ 21 Proms
Edited by Daniel
Ehrenhaft and David
Levithan
0-439-89029-2

❏ Mistletoe: Four
Holiday Stories
By Hailey Abbott,
Melissa de la Cruz,
Aimee Friedman, and
Nina Malkin
0-439-86368-6